Witch City:

Salem In Love

By Julia E. Christian

Julia E. Christian

Copyright © 2025 Julia E. Christian

Cover design by: Louisa Galstyan

Edited by: Victoria Straw and Imogen Evans.

ISBN: 979-8-218-91676-3

Printed in the United States of America

For Herby:

My favorite Salem tour guide.

Chapter 1

June 2024

"I think it's happening tonight," I whisper, popping my head over the top of Stacy's cubicle. She looks up from her computer, eyes wide.

"Freya Whitney, don't mess with me. Are you sure?"

"Pretty sure. He asked me to go out to dinner tonight—and we *never* go out midweek." I swing around the partition and perch on the edge of her desk.

"That's promising. Where's he taking you?" she asks with intrigue, spinning her chair toward me, her inbox fully abandoned.

"La Mercerie." The grin spreading across my face is impossible to stop.

Stacy gasps. "Okay, that's fancy."

"I know, right? And he was *nervous* when he asked. Jackson never gets nervous."

She raises her brows. "That man is pure SoHo cool. This is big."

"I think so, too."

"Oh my God… you're getting engaged!" Stacy jumps up and hugs me so hard I nearly fall off the desk.

"Shhh! He doesn't know I'm onto him," I whisper, quickly scanning the crowded office just in case. As a features editor, Jackson never comes down to the reporters' floor unless it's to see me for lunch—and only if he's not bogged down with edits—but still.

"What's going on over here?" Amanda, Jackson's assistant, pops her head up from the opposite cubicle wall. She must be down here to get him some coffee, or maybe something from one of the other reporters.

"Freya's getting engaged!" Stacy blurts.

"I *might* be getting engaged," I correct quickly, but Stacy waves me off.

"Please, of course you are. And about time too. I thought he was gonna do it on your anniversary last spring."

I laugh to hide the embarrassment that it's been over four years of dating with no ring.

Amanda rounds the corner and joins us, eyes lit up. "Wow, that's exciting!"

I nod, my cheeks already flushing. "Please, don't say anything to him. I don't want him to think I know." She makes a gesture to wordlessly say that her lips are sealed.

"Did you meet here at the magazine?" Amanda asks.

"You don't know the story? Ugh, it's *so* cute," Stacy cuts in, basically bouncing in her seat. "Freya, tell her."

I laugh. "We'd known each other as work acquaintances for a little over a year. I started here fresh out of college, and he always seemed... cool, mature, intimidating."

"Then Freya and I became friends," Stacy jumps in, "and I wanted to set her up with someone so we could go on double dates. And my boyfriend at the time, now husband..." She lifts up her left hand, flashing her giant diamond ring and studded band.

"You just can't help yourself, can you?" I joke, giving her a knowing smile, and the girls laugh. Stacy and Tom just got married last month, and she has no qualms with dropping that piece of information whenever she finds an opening. Of course, I'm happy for her, but I can't help the small part of me that feels jealous I'm not there yet.

"Anyway," Stacy continues, "we set up this blind date with one of Tom's friends from grad school—"

"At White Oak Tavern," I finish.

"In the Village," she confirms.

"Ooh, I love that place," Amanda chimes in.

"Right? So I go to the bar, I'm waiting, but this guy never shows up—"

"Tom found out later that he gave him the wrong time," Stacy whispers quickly to Amanda.

"Didn't matter though. Because just as I'm sitting there thinking I've been stood up, Jackson walks in and asks if he can sit with me. Turns out he liked me too. And…"

"And now you're finally getting engaged!" Stacy exclaims for the third time, and Amanda jumps in to celebrate with her. This time, I don't stop them. I let myself join in on their excitement—because, honestly, I can't hide my joy anymore.

***

After work, I rush home to Jackson and my apartment and spend over an hour getting ready. He had texted me before the end of the day to let me know he would be working a little late and would meet me at the restaurant. I don't mind, though. Nothing can bring me down tonight.

I put on my best gold jewelry, style my hair into the loose waves I know he loves, spritz on his favorite perfume, and slip into a stunning tea-length black dress by Oscar De La Renta. As I stand in front of the full-length mirror, doing one last check, a tiny flicker of doubt worms its way into my thoughts. What if I'm wrong? What if this is just another dinner date, nothing more? But I shake the thought away, forcing a smile at my reflection. Tonight is the night that changes everything. I can feel it.

When I arrive at the restaurant, Jackson is already seated. As the host leads me to the table, I take a moment to observe him from afar. His dirty blonde hair is perfectly combed, and he wears a sleek navy blue suit. When he sees me approach, he stands and greets me with a brief kiss, telling me I look beautiful. I smile, whispering a quick "thank you" before sitting down and grabbing the wine list.

"Have you ordered yet?" I ask, scanning the menu for something celebratory. "We could get a bottle if you want."

"Freya, I cheated on you."

The words hang in the air, thick and suffocating. It feels like the entire restaurant goes silent, though I know it's just my mind going numb. My heart beats in my ears. I look up from the menu, meeting his gaze across the table. His brown eyes are glazed, filled with pity, but there's no sign of guilt.

I swallow hard, trying to steady my voice. "You… what?"

"I'm so sorry, Freya," he says quietly, though his voice lacks the remorse I'm searching for. "It just happened. I couldn't control it."

I let out a shaky breath, the tears threatening to spill. "Who is she?" The words come out sharper than I intend, but I don't care.

"I don't want to get into that," he starts, but I cut him off, my voice rising.

"*Who is she?*" I demand louder than I meant to. The people at the table next to us glance over, their curiosity piqued.

"It's Amanda," he finally admits, looking down at the table.

A sharp, bitter laugh escapes my lips. "Amanda. Amanda, your assistant? Amanda who I have met countless times, who has been to our apartment? *That* Amanda?" Anger flares inside me, hot and relentless. I think back to our conversation this afternoon, and her fake excitement over a proposal she knew wasn't coming.

"Listen, Freya, I don't want to make this harder than it has to be—" he begins, but I cut him off again.

"Well, maybe you shouldn't have cheated on me then!" I shout, loud enough to cause the waiter, who was approaching our table, to quickly turn on his heels and retreat. "And with your assistant? God, Jackson, that's so cliché." The words burn in my chest as I throw the final dig. The betrayal stings, but the fact that it's with *her* is the cherry on top. I feel like an absolute fool.

"I love her, Freya."

His words are quiet, almost apologetic, but there's no conviction behind them.

I scoff, shaking my head in disbelief. "Well then, why don't you marry her?" The words slip out before I can stop them, an attempt to dull the growing pain inside—it doesn't work. Lashing out never does, although that always seems to be my first instinct when I'm hurt. I push my chair back and grab my purse.

"Freya, please. Let's talk about this…" He stands, trying to follow me, but I spin around to face him. I stand inches from him in the middle of the restaurant, my breath shaky.

"There's nothing to talk about. I'll be out of the apartment by the end of the week." With that, I turn and walk toward the door, not looking back. This time, he doesn't follow.

As I step onto the sidewalk, the tears I've been holding back finally fall. How could I have been so stupid? Deep down, I must have known this was coming. A guy like Jackson could never love someone like me.

He's everything I'm not—confident, effortlessly cool, the kind of person who lights up every room without even trying. He has that relaxed charm, that easy smile, which makes people lean in closer when he speaks. And me? I always feel like background noise. Too awkward, too unsure, too much, and somehow never enough all at once. I can't tell if I'm angrier at him for leaving or angrier at myself for letting him slip away.

I turn right, walking past the subway entrance I would normally use to head home. But that isn't home for me anymore. Just then, my phone buzzes in my purse. I pull it out, expecting to see Jackson's name. As I'm about to reject the call, I realize it's not Jackson who's calling me.

"Lindsey!" I practically shout into the phone after answering.

"Hey, Frey! How are you? Feels like it's been forever since we talked." Lindsey's voice cuts through the chaos in my head, and I almost collapse at the sound of it. I can't hold it in anymore, and I burst into sobs, my body shaking.

"Freya? What's going on?" she asks immediately, her concern evident.

"I... Jackson cheated on me." The words tumble out. If it were anyone else, I might have hesitated to share. But not with Lindsey. I know I can tell her anything, and she'll never judge me. She's been my rock since I met her almost ten years ago in our freshman-year dorm.

"Holy shit. Tell me everything."

I walk through the streets of SoHo, phone pressed to my ear, pouring out the whole story. Halfway back to the apartment, I get a text from Jackson saying he'll stay at Amanda's for the week to give me space while I pack. A heavy sigh of relief escapes me. I'm not sure how I would have managed to be in the same apartment as him, pretending everything was fine while I packed up half of the life we used to share.

"I should've known something was wrong," I admit to Lindsey, closing the front door behind me and kicking off my heels. "He's been distant for months. I guess I was in denial. I actually thought a proposal would fix everything."

"Lots of couples go through rough periods," she tries to comfort me, but it doesn't work.

"Not us," I say, laughing bitterly. "I can't even say that anymore. There is no us." The weight of those words crashes over me. I collapse onto the couch, exhaustion pulling at me.

"I'm so sorry, Freya. I'm here for you, you know that. And you can always come to visit me in Salem. You have an open invitation!" Lindsey says, her tone loving and sweet.

"Thanks, Linds. You don't know how much that means to me." I pause, wiping my eyes. "I'm sorry I haven't been the greatest friend lately. I know I haven't called in a while. I've been so wrapped up in work—and... well, Jackson."

"Don't apologize! I know you're always there for me, just like I am for you. Even when we don't talk for a while," she says with a smile I can almost hear.

"I think I'm gonna crash. I have to start packing tomorrow... Maybe I should take a personal day. I don't know what I'm going to do about work." I sink deeper into the couch, my hand still gripping the phone, thinking about the inevitability of running into Jackson at the office.

"You're strong, Freya. You can handle this. Don't forget that." Her voice is steady, grounding. "Get some sleep. Call me if you need me. My last class gets out at three tomorrow, so I'm free after that."

"Thanks again, Linds. Love you."

"Love you too."

The line goes quiet, and I drop the phone beside me on the couch. The apartment, once my safe place, now feels cold and unfamiliar—like I've never truly belonged here.

I guess, in the end, I was right. Tonight did change everything.

Chapter 2

July 2024

If there's one thing I've learned after getting cheated on, dumped, and forced out of my apartment, it's that moving back in with your parents at twenty-eight is like pouring alcohol on a paper cut—you think it can't get worse, but oh, it can.

Packing up the remnants of my life in a SoHo penthouse and dragging them back to my childhood home on the Upper East Side felt like the final blow. Rock bottom, meet Freya Whitney. Living with your parents at this age is humiliating enough. Living with *my* parents? A special kind of hell.

My family has always felt like a completed puzzle, and I'm the extra piece tossed in by mistake. Sure, we may share the same sharp cheekbones and designer taste, but that's where the similarities end. They click together perfectly, an infuriatingly seamless masterpiece. Me? I'm just there, rattling around in the box, hoping someone notices I don't fit.

The Whitneys are a part of the New York socialite circle. My father, Mark, runs a private equity firm and probably loves his money more than he's ever loved another person. My mother, Miranda, is what you'd call a full-time trophy wife. Formerly a stay-at-home mom, now a professional brunch planner and wine-sipping gossip machine. She traded in diapers for Dior and never looked back.

Then there are the golden children. Josie, my older sister, married a banker at twenty-five, popped out two kids, and lives just down the street so she can be on-call for all of Mom's events and breakdowns. Scott, the oldest, works for Dad and is being groomed to take over the firm like a prince waiting for his throne.

And finally, there's me. The youngest. The mistake they won't admit to—because that wouldn't be good for their image at the yacht club. But I've always known. I see it in the way my dad blinks when I walk into a room, like he's just remembered he has a third child. I hear it in my mother's voice every time she critiques my clothes, my career, my life—as if I'm a project that keeps failing inspection.

The thing is, it wasn't always like this. I have memories of warmth from childhood—fleeting, buried, but real. Of Mom humming while she braided my hair before school, of Dad letting me sit in his office chair and pretend to take work calls, of late-night kitchen dance parties with Josie and Scott when we were too wired to sleep. For a while, I believed I was just like them, that I belonged in the Whitney family like any other piece of our shiny, picture-perfect life.

But somewhere along the way, something shifted. As I got older, the warmth faded. I don't know if they grew tired of pretending or if I just stopped fitting their mold. It was like they'd decided I was… extra. Unwanted. An afterthought they didn't know what to do with. I told myself it was because I was different. Too emotional. Too outspoken. Too *me*.

So I tried to change. I straightened my spine and my hair. I smiled more, spoke less. I chose a "respectable" career, though not the one they were hoping for. I played the part. But no matter how much I morphed into someone I thought they wanted, it never felt like enough. Probably because I always knew I could never really be that person.

Someone who cared about money and status above all else. Eventually, I stopped trying to be part of their world and started wondering who I was outside of it.

Sometimes, I almost feel sorry for them. They wouldn't last a week without luxury skincare, imported cheese, or whatever overpriced bottle of wine pairs best with delusion. They can't help it. They're a product of their wealthy and overindulgent environment.

But then again, I might be the same product. After all, they raised me. Their world shaped me. And no matter how hard I try to break away, I see those little reflections of them in myself, just enough to scare the hell out of me.

It's like there are two versions of me living in the same body. One who bends over backward for their approval, reshaping her life into something they'll tolerate just so I can feel like I belong. And the other who wants to cut ties completely, toss the pearls, and disappear into a world where nobody cares about last names or legacy. I'm not sure I trust either version. One's desperate. The other's delusional. And I'm stuck somewhere in between.

"Freya! Dinner is almost ready. Are you joining us tonight?" my mother's voice shrieks up from the first floor, slicing clean through my existential spiral.

"Yes!" I call back from my bed. Well, *used* to be my bed. When I left for college, I moved out for good. Now my old room has been turned into a guest suite.

I stare at my phone for a second before tossing it facedown on the bed. The texts that just buzzed in from Lindsey reads:

Lindsey
Did you tell them yet??
Don't make me come down there and do it for you.

The thought of Lindsey showing up in a puff of smoke just to confront my mother is almost enough to make me smile. Almost.

I haven't told them. Not yet.

How do you announce to your parents that you're abandoning everything they've ever wanted for you—everything you've spent your entire adult life trying to convince yourself *you* wanted too—for a place you've never even visited?

You don't. You avoid it until it absolutely can't be avoided anymore.

It's only been a couple of weeks since Lindsey called and offered me the spare room in her Salem apartment.

"Come stay with me." She begged over the phone. "You need a reset, and Salem is magic—literally and metaphorically."

Her longtime roommate, Charlene, had just moved in with her girlfriend, and the second the words "I'll keep the rent cheap" left Lindsey's mouth, I felt something in my chest loosen for the first time in weeks. I heard myself say "yes" before I could even think through the decision.

Thankfully, I was able to find a new job in Salem pretty fast, much to Stacy's dismay. Last week, she tried to convince me to stay in New York and keep working at the magazine.

"This is just a small bump for you guys. You'll work it out and be back together in no time," she said, petting my hair as I slumped miserably over my desk. That was the first day after the breakup that I'd finally mustered enough courage to go back to work.

"I need you here. How will I ever brave New York without you?" she finished with a whine.

I knew what that really meant, though: *How will I ever brave New York's social scene without you and your door-opening, VIP-securing last name?*

This wasn't new to me. I lost a little faith in our friendship that day.

The new job is at a slightly less impressive publication than the one I'm at now, and I'll be taking a small pay cut, but I won't have to see Jackson every day or pretend that everything is fine when it's not. That alone is worth more than the salary drop.

Of course, none of this will make any sense to my parents. As I descend the stairs to face them in the dining room, I know I'm about to be in for it.

The table is set for five. It always is, as if Josie and Scott might magically appear out of thin air and bless us with their presence. My mother places a linen napkin on her lap like she's about to be interviewed for *Town & Country* magazine. My father is still scrolling through work emails, his Bluetooth permanently lodged in his right ear.

I sit down in my seat and clear my throat. "So... I have some news."

No reaction. Just the faint clink of cutlery.

"I'm moving," I say, then pause. "To Salem. Massachusetts."

My father finally looks up. My mother freezes mid-sip of her chardonnay.

"Salem?" Mom says slowly as if she's testing the syllables. "As in... witches and broomsticks, Salem?"

"I mean, yeah. But also cobblestone streets, seaside charm? That Salem. I'm moving in with Lindsey."

"But it is where they burned all those witches, right?" she adds with a grimace.

"They didn't burn them. They hanged them," I say, and then shake my head. "Anyway, it's a perfectly normal town now. I think."

"Why would you go there?" my dad asks, skeptical. "What about your job?"

"I was offered a position as a columnist at a newspaper in Salem," I tell them, trying to sound casual. "It pays less, but it's a much better fit for me."

Dad raises an eyebrow, skeptical as usual. "What's the paper?"

"*The Harbor Light*," I say. "It's a small, independent paper that focuses on local culture and social justice. You know, human-interest stories."

His face scrunches in confusion. "Never heard of it. Why would you give up your position as a political reporter to take a lower-paying job writing about—what...? Local bake sales and knitting clubs?"

"Actually, I'll be writing about real people doing things that make a difference in their communities," I reply, rolling my eyes. "Things that actually matter. Not sleazy politicians bribing their way to the top. Plus, I won't have to see Jackson every day."

My mother sighs. "You're really still upset about that breakup?"

"It wasn't just a breakup. He cheated on me. He's in love with someone else." My throat burns slightly when the words come out.

She waves a dismissive hand. "Men make mistakes, Freya. It doesn't mean you throw your entire life away."

"I'm not throwing it away," I say, sharper than I mean to. "I'm starting over. I'm twenty-eight and I've never made a single choice just for me. Until now."

My mother makes a face like she's just bitten into a lemon. "But Freya, your whole life is here. Your job. Your friends. Your... history."

"That's kind of the point," I mutter.

My father crosses his arms. "So you're throwing away a perfectly good career track to play house in some New England tourist trap? With Lindsey, of all people?"

I bristle. "Yes. With Lindsey. You remember her—Columbia, straight A's, kind and caring human being?"

My mother lets out a soft gasp. "Darling, don't get defensive. We just want what's best for you. And frankly, that doesn't involve moving to a town with fake witches and crazy people."

Dad cuts in. "Didn't she major in theater or something?"

I let out a long sigh, trying to center myself. "Yes. She's a music teacher now, and she owns a really cute apartment near the harbor. It's a good situation. No crazy people involved."

Mom purses her lips. "Honestly, Freya, how do you think this will look? People will talk."

That makes me laugh. "God forbid the Upper East Side learns I left Manhattan for a town full of crystal shops and psychics."

"There's still time to fix this," she says. "Maybe call Jackson. Apologize. He comes from a good family—"

That's the moment it clicks. The final nail in the coffin. They don't actually care about what I want, what's best for me. They never have. I grip the edge of the table, steadying myself.

"I'm not doing this," I say as I stand. "I'm not staying here just so you can keep pretending I fit into your version of a perfect life."

"Freya," my father warns, like I'm a child misbehaving in public.

But I'm already walking out of the room.

***

Back upstairs, I fall onto the bed and grab my phone. Another text from Lindsey lights up the screen.

Lindsey
Told them yet??

Do I need to bring wine or emotional support snacks when I pick you up at the airport next weekend?

I smile, then type back:

Freya
Both. Definitely both.

My suitcase is open at the foot of the bed, half full. I push myself off the mattress and pull my dresser drawer open to grab another pile of clothes to drop in.

This isn't just an escape. It's a reclamation—of a life that hasn't been my own for a very long time.

I glance out the window. The skyline is still the same—glassy, glittering, unreachable.

And for the first time in my life, I don't want to chase it anymore.

Chapter 3

If there's one thing I've learned since moving to Salem, Massachusetts, it's that no matter how far you run, your problems always have a way of following you… they're annoyingly good at keeping up.

It's been three days since I left my entire life behind in New York, and I honestly can't tell if I'm any better for it. I'm hundreds of miles away from my family and my ex, and I feel just as shitty as I did back in Manhattan. And maybe even more alone.

I sit cross-legged on the floor at the foot of my bed, half-unpacking, half-spiraling, when I hear the front door of Lindsey's apartment—*our* apartment—creak open, followed by the familiar earthquake thud as it slams shut.

"Freya?!" she calls.

"In my room!" I yell back.

Lindsey comes barreling in, the same bundle of chaotic energy she's always been.

"So weird to hear you call this 'your room.' Feels like we're back in the dorms," she says cheerfully, flopping onto my unmade bed.

"Yeah, minus the gross furniture, the mold in the bathroom, and all the booze." I laugh.

"Hey! *We still have the booze,*" she counters, grinning.

Lindsey is exactly the same as she was at Columbia: bubbly, excitable, and fiercely loyal. Adjusting to living with her again has been the easiest part of this whole move. Her support has been my saving grace.

The past few days have been a montage of catching up on our lives, reminiscing about school adventures, reviving old inside jokes, and watching romantic comedies until we pass out on the couch. We've fallen right back into our old rhythm—except now we're twenty-eight, with jobs and bills and the kind of responsibilities that used to feel like other people's problems. Adulthood sucks.

Lindsey and I met our freshman year at Columbia, and she has always been the kind of person who makes choices based on joy instead of obligation. She changed her major more often than I changed moisturizers and still managed to graduate with a musical theater degree and a permanent skip in her step. I never understood how someone so chaotic could still seem so... certain.

After college, she moved back to Salem, just like she said she would. It's her hometown, and her parents still live here. She's close with them in a way I'll never be with mine. They supported every major change and every crazy dream, and they were over the moon when she landed her job as the music teacher at her old high school.

Lindsey used to come to my family's house for the holidays when she couldn't afford to fly home during college. Selfishly, I loved having her there. She was a buffer, someone to absorb the pressure of our dinner conversations, to distract my parents with her stories and charm. She made things easier.

She always has.

And now she's given me a place to land when I have nowhere else to go. Not out of pity, not to play the hero, just because that's who she is. Lindsey has this quiet, unwavering sort of kindness, the kind that doesn't ask questions or keep score. Honestly, I don't think I've ever met anyone like her.

The second-floor apartment on Carlton Street is small but in a cute, quaint, seaside-town kind of way. Nestled tightly in one of the historical pockets of Salem, it fits right in with the whimsical vibe of the city, with the dark wood floors, brick fireplace, secondhand Persian rugs, and mismatched upholstered furniture that Lindsey has collected over the years.

I never imagined myself living in a place like this. But I think that's exactly why I like it. Every apartment I had in Manhattan after graduation was newly built and so luxurious it bordered on ridiculous—marble floors, ornate crown moldings, top-of-the-line appliances, and the most expensive matching furniture sets money could buy. All things, I'm starting to realize, I never really needed... and probably never even wanted. I'm ready for a change. I'm ready to live in a place that feels a little more *me*. Whatever that may be.

Lindsey kicks her shoes off and stretches her long, slim body out on my bed, her dark hair fanning out on my pillow.

"Make yourself at home, why don't you? Can I get you anything? Nice herbal tea, some relaxing music?" I tease with a chuckle.

"No, I'm all set, thanks! So this is how you're spending your Saturday?" she asks, gesturing to the chaotic explosion of clothes, books, and trinkets that have taken over my floor.

I nod. "I'm trying to get through the last of these boxes while I still have some free time. I start work Monday, and I want to feel settled before then."

If I don't finish unpacking now, my brain will be too cluttered to focus on anything else this week. I want to make a good impression. New job, new coworkers, new me… right?

"Well, you have until eight to do what you need to do, and then we're going out." She says in a tone that is not to be argued with. "And don't even try to get out of it. You've been here for three days, and you haven't met any of my friends yet! I promise it's a really fun crew. None of them bite… unless you ask Damon super nicely."

I let out a chuckle. I *do* want to meet all of Lindsey's friends. She's known most of them since childhood, and she's always spoken so highly of them.

"What's the plan for the evening?" I ask.

"Well," Lindsey starts, speeding up like she's afraid I'll stop her, "you might think this is super lame, but you're not allowed to say no. We're giving you the full Salem experience."

"Oh God, just tell me what the plan is. You're making me nervous," I say, crushing an empty box. My mind drifts to some of the wild scenarios Lindsey had gotten us into during college. I can only guess what kind of plans she's cooking up now.

"We're going on a ghost tour!" she says excitedly. "I swear it's not as hokey as it sounds. We walk all around town, and you get to learn a lot about Salem's history… Plus, one of our good friends is the tour guide, so we get a discount."

Honestly? That's tamer than I expected. Lindsey's college plans usually involved sneaking into concerts or accidentally joining a frat. I guess the years have mellowed her out.

Still, the cynic in me can't help but hesitate when the words 'ghost' and 'tour' come out of her mouth together.

I let out a sigh and unzip a suitcase that is bursting at the seams with clothes. "Uhhh… I don't know, Linds. I've still got a ton to do and—"

"Please, please, please! It'll be way more fun if you're there," she begs.

I glance up at her with a dubious look on my face. I know that she loves Salem's 'spooky side,' but a ghost tour seems too far-reaching and cliché for me. I don't believe in the supernatural. I believe in what I can see with my own two eyes. But I swallow my pride for Lindsey's sake. I know she really wants me to come, and I could never say no to her after all the kindness she has shown me.

"All right, all right. I surrender. I'll come…" I say, pushing myself up from the floor. Lindsey shrieks and launches off the bed, pulling me into a dramatic hug that nearly knocks me over.

"Oh yay, yay, yay! I'm so excited," she screams.

"But only because I want to hang out with you and your friends," I warn. "I'm not saying I'm going to enjoy the… ghost thing or whatever," I add, and she laughs a little.

"I know you probably won't believe any of it. But just give it a chance, for me. You might have fun," she says with a wink. Lindsey is always so patient with me and my misgivings.

I smile despite myself. "Anything for you. Are we at least going to a bar after?"

"Duh, of course. Who do you think we are?" Lindsey quips back.

I let out a little chuckle. "Don't know why I ever doubted you."

***

I quickly fall in step behind Lindsey's long strides. She's at least five inches taller than me, so keeping up without losing my breath feels like a cardio workout. We're practically jogging now, weaving through the Saturday night crowds in a race to reach the meeting spot for the tour on time.

Salem is buzzing with chaotic energy—people of all sorts laughing, strolling, snapping photos, skipping across cobblestone streets under the pink glow of the setting sun. We're just a small part of the current sweeping through the historic district.

"Okay, hold on. They should be around here. Let me text Charlene," Lindsey says, slowing down as she pulls out her phone. I step ahead of her and finally take the chance to catch my breath, pulling my blonde hair up into a ponytail to relieve some of the heat clinging to my neck. Even in jean shorts and a tank top, I'm sweltering in the thick July humidity.

Now that we're not moving as fast, I have a moment to take in my surroundings. A warm, amber glow spills out from shop windows lining both sides of the pedestrian street we're walking down. A crooked little street sign up ahead tells me it's called Essex Street. By the looks of it, most of the shops we pass have something to do with witches. Whimsical names like The Coven's Cottage, The Magic Parlor, and Wynott's Wands remind me that I am no longer in New York City. It honestly surprises me that all these shops can coexist, one right after the other, without any competition. But then I remember that Salem is famous for its tourists and busy Halloween season. I can't help but wonder how many of these stores are open just to take advantage of that.

I'm deep in thought as I continue walking, eyeing a flyer for a psychic taped to a lamp post, when I crash—*hard*—into a solid wall of a man. The impact knocks me backward, and I instinctively reach out, trying to steady myself. Instead, I end up dragging the poor guy down with me. We hit the ground in a tangled heap, me flat on my back and him landing squarely on top of me.

"Oh my God, I'm so sorry, I didn't—" I start, breathless and scrambling to make sense of what just happened. But the words die in my throat the second I look up and meet a pair of piercing green eyes belonging to the man who is currently pressed up against me in the middle of the street.

Before I can fully register what's happening, Lindsey comes running up from behind us, "Are you guys okay?!" she asks, already grabbing the man's arm to help him up before offering me a hand.

"We're okay. Just a little tumble," the man says with a small smirk. He looks back at me and reaches up to the side of my face. His fingers comb through my hair as he picks a small leaf from the strands and throws it to the ground. His touch is surprisingly gentle. I let out a small breath and dust myself off.

"Looked like more than a tumble from where I was watching," Lindsey teases, slightly out of breath. The man chuckles and pulls her into a hug.

I blink. Wait—she *knows* this guy?

As they pull apart, I glance around and notice a crowd of about twenty people watching us, many of them holding little paper booklets. Right. The walking tour. Lindsey's friend. The tour guide. Which must mean that this guy—this human mountain I just steamrolled—is *the* friend.

Realization sets in, along with a wave of mortification, and I scramble to recover.

"I'm so sorry. You must be the tour guide. It's really nice to meet you. I'm Freya Whitney, Lindsey's roommate." I awkwardly extend a hand.

He takes it, shaking firmly. I feel a subtle jolt at the contact—maybe static electricity or maybe my nerves. "Nice to meet you, Freya. I'm Liam Doyle. No apologies necessary. Why don't you both join us in the back?"

His smile is disarming. I return it, still a little dazed, and follow Lindsey as we ease into the crowd.

We join a few of Lindsey's other friends, including someone I actually recognize, Charlene. She's dressed in a sleek black top and a trendy miniskirt, effortlessly stylish despite her wedge heels, which seem like an odd choice for a walking tour. She had visited Lindsey a few times during college, and we always hit it off, but I haven't seen her since.

"Hey, girl! So good to see you again," Charlene whispers, pulling me into a quick hug.

"You too! You look amazing," I whisper back, just as someone in the group shushes us. We trade amused glances. "Where's Jenna tonight?" I ask, realizing her girlfriend is missing.

"She couldn't make it out tonight. But don't worry, you'll meet her soon," Charlene replies before turning her attention back to Liam.

"All right, now that everyone's settled," Liam says, facing the group, "my name's Liam, and I'll be your guide tonight…"

He launches into a brief intro as he walks backward, leading us slowly down Essex Street. "I was born and raised here in Salem. My family's been here since the town was first settled. I'm a practicing Wiccan, taught by my parents, I majored in History at Salem State, and I have a master's in Folklore and Mythology, as well. Oh, and I'm a Scorpio sun, so when it comes to the occult, I know my stuff."

The group chuckles at the wink he adds. He's charming, I'll give him that. And if it weren't for the subject matter, I'd be wrapped in every word his smooth, deep voice had to say. However, I'm not following any of it.

My first impression of Liam, the one that found him intriguing and mysterious, is quickly squashed by my second impression. The one that makes me think he must have some loose wires in his head if he really believes in all this supernatural stuff.

After he finishes his introduction, our slightly woo-woo tour guide leads us down a quiet alley, and I lean toward Lindsey. "What's a Wiccan?"

"They're Pagan. Kind of like a modern witch," she says simply.

I raise an eyebrow. "So… your tour guide friend… is a witch?"

She laughs. "Sort of. Ask him about it sometime! It's actually pretty interesting."

Before I can respond with another sarcastic quip, Lindsey gestures to the two guys walking ahead of us. "Freya, these are our other friends—Damon and Bailey."

I smile and quickly wave, saying, "Hey! So nice to finally meet you guys."

"Likewise! We've heard a lot about you," Damon says, falling in step next to me.

"All good things, I hope," I joke, though I glance at Lindsey for reassurance. Knowing her, I'm sure she's told them some stories about our time at school, and I'm hoping none of those stories had to do with my family. I don't want her friends to have any preconceived notions about me based on my upbringing.

"Oh, of course! And I see you met Liam," Damon adds with a smirk, gesturing toward the front of the group.

"Briefly," I say, letting out an awkward laugh.

"He's a good guy. You'll love him—big teddy bear under all those tattoos," he says, waving his hand as if to tell me not to worry.

Damon's got a round middle, short blonde hair with matching scruff, and a laid-back energy that puts me at ease. Bailey, beside him, is taller and quieter, with warm brown curls and caramel skin. His shoulders slump forward slightly as if he isn't used to his own stature. He offers a kind smile when I say hello. They both seem nice, and I'm relieved by that. I'm just hoping that Lindsey's friends like me. I can't quite tell yet if they do.

Before we can chat more, Liam stops the group in front of a busy restaurant and turns to face us.

"Behind me is Turner's Seafood," he announces. "Amazing food. If you like lobster scampi or steak tips, this place is a must. Sadly, I'm not allowed to expense a group meal, so instead, I'll share some history and haunting tales."

The group laughs. I can't help but roll my eyes. When I glance back up to where Liam stands up front, our gazes meet. Had he already been looking at me? I offer a small smile, but he doesn't return it. Instead, his expression is stiff—and a little cold, if I'm being honest. Then he looks away and launches back into his spiel. I decide not to overthink the brief, awkward moment and write it off as a misread on my part. At least, that's what I hope it is.

"The land we're standing on used to belong to Bridget Bishop. It was the site of her apple orchard during the mid to late 1600s. Her ownership ended in June of 1692 when she became the first person executed for witchcraft during the Salem Witch Trials."

I've never heard of Bridget Bishop. Come to think of it, I don't think I could name a single other person who was executed during the Witch Trials. Thinking back to childhood, I remember learning about the event in history class a little bit. And by *a little bit*, I mean I was vaguely aware it happened. Kids in Salem must have a completely different perspective, growing up practically inside living history. I was never really one for history.

Liam continues, "Over the years after the Witch Trials, the land was used for a variety of things. The building itself was constructed in 1831. Back then, it was called Lyceum Hall, and it hosted political lectures and cultural presentations. By 1973, it was converted into a restaurant and pub, and it's stayed that way in a few different forms ever since—Turner's being the most recent adaptation. Even though Bridget didn't own the land for very long, patrons and staff still see her around the restaurant's dining room and kitchens from time to time…"

As Liam continues to speak, I can't help but become mesmerized by him; his words, his voice, his intonation. This is also the first moment I really take in his appearance, and I have to admit to myself that he *is* an attractive man. Or witch. Witch-man.

He's at least six feet tall. Probably taller, considering how much I had to crane my neck to meet his eyes—and I'm not even that short at five feet six. His dark, shaggy hair almost falls into his eyes but is cut just neatly enough to seem intentional. His face is thin, and his nose is prominent, but not in a way that distracts. I can tell he works out, both from looking at his lean but strong physique and from the solidness of his chest that I felt earlier. Scattered across his arms are so many tattoos I wouldn't even be able to start counting them. But mostly, I can't look away from his eyes. Bright, striking green. Almost turquoise. It's not a color you often see in someone's eyes, which is probably why I am so captivated by them.

"All right! We're going to head across the parking lot behind you to our next destination—The Old Salem Jail," Liam says, yanking me out of my daydream. I realize I was so distracted that I must have missed him talking about the actual hauntings at Turner's. Not that I would have believed him anyway.

We continue walking with the group, staying toward the back. Liam is already being bombarded with questions from tourists at the front of the pack.

"So interesting. I forgot about those stories. We should have dinner there again soon," Charlene says to us. The others nod in agreement.

My brows scrunch. I can't help but ask, "Do you guys actually… believe in all this stuff?" Honestly, though, I think I already know the answer.

"Yeah, pretty much. When you grow up around here, it's kind of embedded in your DNA," Charlene says with a little laugh.

"That's not true at all! I grew up here just like you, and I don't necessarily believe in ghosts," Damon chimes in defensively.

Charlene scoffs. "Oh, please. This coming from the man who refuses to walk past Howard Street Cemetery now because you thought something followed you home last month."

"Okay, listen. I took a shortcut through there *one time*. And now all the kitchen cabinets open by themselves in the middle of the night. What do you have to say to *that*, huh?" Damon shoots back confidently.

"I say you have a roommate who stays up past three in the morning playing video games every night," Charlene retorts.

Damon turns to Bailey, clearly looking for backup. Bailey looks at him, hesitates for a second, then shrugs.

"The first time I left a few of them open, it was an accident. But then you freaked out the next morning, and I thought it was funny. So now I leave them open every once in a while to keep you on your toes," Bailey says casually like it's a conversation they've had a dozen times.

"Well. I have to say, I'm feeling pretty betrayed right now," Damon says, deadpan and dramatic.

Lindsey and I laugh. Charlene cuts in before Damon can continue.

"The *point* is, we might not all believe in poltergeists or haunted dolls or vengeful nuns rising from the dead… well, I guess I can't speak for Damon. But most of us can tell the difference between what's real and what isn't. That said, we do believe in something—spirits, souls, energy, however you want to phrase it. And growing up with Liam probably had something to do with that, too." She gestures toward the front, where Liam is still leading the group.

"Huh," I say, turning her words over in my mind.

"Do you believe in anything beyond the physical world you see around you?" she asks gently. I can tell by her tone she's not being judgmental, she's genuinely curious. Guilt flares in my chest as I realize *my* question earlier didn't come from that same place. Mine had come with a tinge of judgment. And, if I'm honest, that judgment is still buried somewhere inside me. I hate that.

I think for a moment before responding. "I mean… not really. How could I believe in something when I haven't seen any proof that it actually exists?"

"Freya's never been around this kind of stuff before," Lindsey jumps in. "It's hard for her to wrap her head around it all, but she'll come around eventually. We just have to convince her, that's all." She bumps her shoulder against mine playfully. Once again, she's seeing the best in me, even when I'm showing my worst.

"Oh, totally!" Charlene says. "You'll feel the Salem magic soon enough. It just takes a second for the newcomers. Right, Bailey?" She glances at him before turning back to me. "Bailey moved here for college. He and Liam were roommates their freshman year."

Bailey lets out a low hum. "Get a couple drinks in me, then I'll start to feel the Salem magic."

Charlene laughs and throws an arm around his shoulders as they walk a few steps ahead. It's a sweet gesture, from both her and Lindsey. Their way of welcoming me in, of trying to make me feel like I belong here.

But I'm pretty doubtful that I'll ever truly believe in the "Salem magic." Because magic isn't real. If it were, I'd have my fairy godmother, my happily ever after, and someone who loved me enough to choose me over his assistant.

Liam finally stops the group in front of a large building about six stories tall. It looks like some kind of office building. While I don't believe it's full of ghosts, I'm not too proud to admit that it definitely gives off a creepy vibe.

"This is the Old Salem Jail," Liam says, gesturing up at the building. "I know it doesn't look like much now, but back in the 1600s, this was where all the people accused of witchcraft were imprisoned until they were either freed or executed.

"Some of the paranormal activity people claim to experience here includes hearing footsteps and disembodied voices, seeing objects fly across rooms, and even witnessing full-body apparitions walking down the third-floor corridor.

"One of the more chilling stories happened when the building functioned as office space for a phone company in the nineties. Office workers constantly reported hearing screaming coming from the other end of phone calls. But when they asked the person they were speaking to if they'd heard it too, the answer was always no."

A few people in the group gasp with fear or fascination, but I can't help letting out a small scoff, paired with yet another eye roll. I don't understand why everyone is eating this up so eagerly.

"Something you want to add, Flora?" Liam asks impatiently. It takes me a second to realize he's talking to me.

"It's Freya," I reply, a little offended he forgot my name. "And no, I didn't mean to interrupt. I just find it a little hard to believe, that's all."

"That's okay. But maybe keep it to yourself next time. You wouldn't want to offend one of the spirits, they might follow you home," Liam says, clearly joking but with a sharp undertone, before launching back into his monologue about the old jail.

"Don't listen to him," Lindsey whispers to me once everyone turns their attention back to Liam. "He just takes all of this really seriously. It *is* his job, after all."

Doesn't make it okay for him to be a dick, I think, but I don't say it out loud. I just force a smile, nod, and turn back to pretend I'm listening.

The rest of the tour goes by relatively quickly. My favorite parts are all the walking in between each stop when I get to chat with Lindsey's friends and start to get to know them better. But whenever the group pauses to hear another story, I tune Liam out and focus on the surrounding trees, the cheesy storefronts, or the people walking by. I've had enough ghost stories for one night, and honestly, I don't think I'll be able to hold back another snarky remark if I do pay attention.

Though, if anyone deserves one more snarky comment, it's definitely Liam—especially after the way he humiliated me in front of an entire group of strangers.

By the time the tour loops back to its starting point—a small house on Essex Street where the company is based—I'm more than ready to find the nearest bar and get a drink. The five of us hang back while Liam wraps up with the stragglers, thanking him and asking final questions. When he finally makes his way over to us, Damon reaches out to shake his hand, pulling him into a quick hug and pat on the back.

"Great tour tonight, man," Damon says.

"Thanks!" Liam replies, clearly glad to be among friends.

"Yeah! Really enjoyed the part where you forgot Freya's name and embarrassed her in front of the whole group," Charlene says, her voice dripping with faux sincerity.

There's a beat of silence.

"It's all in good fun, right, Freya?" Liam asks, his light eyes meeting my dark brown ones. He's trying to play it off like a joke, but I can tell he's still annoyed.

"Right," I respond with a tight-lipped smile.

Another awkward silence hangs over the group for a second before Damon breaks it.

"Not to be dramatic or anything, but if I don't get a beer in my hand within the next five minutes, I *will* pass out from sobriety."

"Aww. And you were afraid you were being dramatic," Charlene shoots back sarcastically as she starts walking away. "C'mon! O'Neill's this way."

We all follow behind her, Bailey and Liam falling into conversation while Damon runs to catch up with Charlene.

"You'll love O'Neill's, Freya! It's a really fun Irish pub, just like the ones we used to go to in New York. And we can do pickleback shots!" Lindsey says, linking our arms together.

"Oh God. I don't know if my body can still handle shots of pure whiskey," I say.

"You'd be surprised…" Lindsey responds with a grin, and we laugh, falling into a quick pace behind the group.

As we walk to the bar, I just pray that the tension between Liam and me will start to fade. Lindsey wouldn't be friends with an asshole, I remind myself.

Boy, could that not be farther from the truth.

Chapter 4

O'Neill's is packed—not that surprising for a Saturday night, though. A ripple of excitement runs through me as the bouncer hands my ID back, and I follow Lindsey inside. I haven't been out to a bar in what feels like forever. I wasn't exactly in a party mood during my last month in New York.

The pub is alive with laughter and chatter, and the air is thick with the smell of liquor and beer. Irish flags hang on the walls beside posters for Guinness and Baileys. To my left, a group of musicians play a lively Irish jig. I watch the fiddle player, mesmerized by how fast his bow moves over the strings.

The bar stretches along the right side of the room, and the rest of the space is crammed with tables and chairs. Toward the back, I spot a pool table and dart boards, all occupied by tipsy patrons. I trail behind the group to the center of the pub, where we push a few high-top tables together.

"What can I get you, Freya?" Bailey asks as I pull my chair in. Someone's shoulder brushes against mine, and I glance over to see none other than Liam dropping into the seat beside me. Not sure how we ended up this close, but I'm silently cursing whatever deity allowed it—because, apparently, that's what people do in Salem.

"We're all starting with picklebacks! No one is arguing!" Lindsey shouts over the noise.

"Uhh, I don't know about that, Lindsey. Some of us have things to do in the morning," Liam replies, his tone smug. For some reason, the fact that he doesn't want to take a shot makes me want to take one that much more.

"Well, I'm in desperate need of a fun night out, so count me in," I say, turning away from the grump on my right.

"Me too!" Charlene chimes in, and Damon raises his hand to agree.

"Yay! Don't worry, Freya—we're going to show you a great time tonight," Lindsey says as she grabs Bailey by his sleeve. "Come on, Bailey, help me grab the shots. You're having one too!"

Bailey follows after her like a lost puppy. "O-Okay. Uh, sure," he stammers as they weave through the crowd. I let out a soft chuckle and turn back to the table.

Across from me, Charlene and Damon are already bickering about something. In the short time I've spent around them, I've noticed they tend to clash often—but in an affectionate way, more sibling-like than anything else.

I shift awkwardly in my seat, realizing Liam is now the only one left to talk to. Great. Still, I figure I might as well try to clear the air. I swallow my pride and turn toward him in some effort to squash the tension between us.

"Hey, Liam. Uh… I'm sorry again about interrupting your tour. I know it's important to you, so I just wanted to apologize."

"It's important to a lot of other people, too. Not just me," he says flatly.

Oof. Obviously, my apology is not accepted.

"Yeah, no… I, uh, I get that. I've seen *Hocus Pocus*," I say with a chuckle, trying to lighten the mood. However, I internally kick myself for the comment when I receive a glare instead of a smile. I sigh. "Look, I'm just trying to say sorry. The least you could do is say, 'It's okay,' so we can move on."

"Well, maybe it isn't okay. And as far as apologies go, yours isn't winning any awards. Come back to me when you genuinely feel bad," he replies, sharp and unforgiving.

I blink at him, stunned. Before I can figure out what to say, Lindsey and Bailey return, setting down two shot glasses in front of each of us.

"All right, everyone, pause your conversations. Time for shots!" Lindsey announces.

"Let's toast to another fabulous ghost tour from the man, the myth, the legend—Liam Doyle!" Damon calls out, raising his glass.

We slam our glasses down, raise them to cheers, then bring them down again before knocking them back. I chase the whiskey with the pickle juice, grateful for how it masks the burn.

"I'm just hoping a real spirit followed Damon home this time. It'd make for a way better story," Charlene teases.

"You better pray it didn't. Otherwise, I'm capturing it and setting it loose in your apartment. Let's see what you say when your kitchen cabinets start opening on their own," Damon says seriously.

"Oh, please. What are you gonna do, use a jerry-rigged vacuum like a fake Ghostbuster?" she shoots back.

"No. Luckily, I happen to know a pretty skilled Wiccan who can whip up a spirit-summoning charm. Or something like that. Right, Liam?" Damon asks with a grin.

"Don't bring that up, D. You wouldn't want to offend Frida over here," Liam replies, pretending to inspect his empty shot glass.

"It's *Freya*. For fuck's sake. And just because I don't believe in something you do doesn't make me a bad person," I snap.

"No, it doesn't," he says evenly. "But mocking people who do believe in it makes you an ignorant one." He turns to face me.

"I wasn't mocking anyone! I was just expressing a little skepticism. And frankly, your 'ghost tour' could use a healthy dose of that." Now I'm getting mad.

"But your skepticism is rooted in your unwillingness to see beyond your own perspective. That's what makes you ignorant," he says calmly.

"Well, if I'm ignorant, then you're deranged." I don't even know why I'm so annoyed. Maybe because he's smug.

Maybe because I know he sees through me, and I don't like how exposed that makes me feel.

He laughs under his breath, but I get the sense he's not amused.

"Exactly what I'd expect from a naive outsider—shallow, condescending remarks about people you don't even know. Maybe don't comment on things you clearly don't understand," he says, eyes locked on mine. "You might think it's all smoke and mirrors, but to some of us, this stuff is real. It's a big part of our lives. It's how we make sense of the world around us, how we cope with loss."

"I was just trying to apologize. But if you want to act like a child, be my guest." I *should've* stopped there. But of course, I didn't. "You act like you were raised by wolves. Oh, wait! Sorry, that's right. You were raised by witches. How could I forget?"

The second the words are released, I want to claw them back. There's a deafening silence that hangs heavily over the group. Liam holds my gaze for a beat longer, then stands up abruptly and walks toward the restrooms.

I turn back to the table. Damon's expression is held in a cringe while Charlene and Lindsey have apologetic looks on their faces. Bailey is avoiding eye contact with me altogether.

"Well… that escalated quickly," I say with a halfhearted chuckle. There's a chance I may have taken things too far.

"Don't worry about it," Lindsey says quickly. "Liam can lose his head a little, sometimes, and he knows how to push people. He's just really passionate about the beliefs he was raised with. Don't hold it against him. He's actually a great guy once you get to know him."

"He shouldn't have started it. You were just trying to apologize," Charlene adds. She starts to rise from her seat. "Let me go talk to him. He should really tell you *he's* sorry."

I hold out a hand to stop her. "No, Charlene, it's okay. Honestly, I'd rather just forget about it and put it behind us."

"You sure?" she asks gently.

"Positive." I was the one who crossed a line, after all.

A few seconds pass in awkward silence until Damon, bless him, jumps in.

"In the spirit of putting it behind us—who wants another shot?" he asks, clearly hoping to smooth over the situation with humor. We all cheer in response.

"I'll help you grab them," I offer, standing up from my seat.

At the bar, we place the order and wait while the bartender lines up shot glasses. Damon glances over at me with a warm smile.

"The girls are right, by the way. Just ignore Liam. He'll come around. Although, maybe skip comparing his family to wolves next time."

"Yeah, noted," I say with a soft laugh. "I just want to make a good impression with you guys. You seem like a really great group of friends, and I feel like I'm blowing it."

"If it's any consolation, I like you. I think you'll fit in just fine."

"You have no idea how much I needed to hear that," I say, returning his smile. More than anything, I just wanted Lindsey's friends to like me—to feel like I could belong in their circle. After how tonight started, I was convinced I'd ruined my chances. But Damon's words give me a flicker of hope.

The bartender hands us both another tray of shots, and we make our way back to the table. As we approach, I can see that Liam has returned, but he isn't sitting in the same seat he was in before. Charlene is now in the chair next to mine, and Liam is on the complete opposite side of the table. I guess they switched seats.

I sit down again, grab another pair of shot glasses, and down them both. The buzz finally starts to kick in, dulling the awful churn in my stomach. I honestly do feel bad. But considering all of this started because I *tried* to apologize, I'm not exactly lining up to try again. If he wants to hold a grudge forever, he's more than welcome to.

"Hope you don't mind if I join you over here," Charlene says with a kind smile.

"Of course not!" I say, happy to play along like this is just a random seat shuffle.

Across the table, Liam is talking to Bailey about something that I can't make out. I hope it has nothing to do with me. It seems like a normal conversation, though. Neither of their facial expressions is warped in disgust or irritation, so that's a good sign, at least.

"So, what do you do for work, Freya?" Damon asks from across the table.

"I'm a journalist. I'm starting work on Monday as a columnist for a small newspaper in town. It's not as well known as the magazine I worked for in New York, pays a little less—but I have more freedom since it's my own column, so I'm looking forward to it." Sometimes, I ramble when I'm nervous, and talking about my recent career move still makes me a little uneasy. Especially after the reaction I got from my parents.

Even my friends in Manhattan thought I was crazy to leave my well-paying reporter job to work for a paper none of them had ever heard of. Or at least I thought they were friends. Maybe not, though, since I haven't heard from any of them since the move. Not even Stacy.

"Whoa, that's awesome. So you're, like, wicked smart, huh?" he teases.

"Sometimes," I reply with a laugh, relieved when he doesn't press me for more details about the change.

Charlene and Damon ask more questions about my work, and I reciprocate, curious about theirs. I find out Charlene's a real estate agent, and Damon's in marketing. Normally, I'd be eager to hear about their lives, but I can't stop my thoughts from drifting back to Liam. I try to stay present, but it's almost impossible. He feels like a storm cloud rolling in on my periphery, ready to ruin a sunny day. And no matter how hard I try, I can't ignore it.

***

As the night wears on, we knock back more shots, swap stories, and let the Irish music swirl around us. I start to feel like I'm actually warming up to everyone in the group, though that might have more to do with how drunk we all are at this point. Still, it's been nice getting to know them a little more personally.

Well, most of them.

Liam has barely looked my way since our little spat earlier, so I'm not exactly expecting any heart-to-hearts from him tonight.

Later on, Damon and Lindsey are playing pool while Bailey and Charlene invite me to join them for a game of darts. Thankfully, Liam stays put at the table, with the excuse that he's guarding our spot.

Works for me.

We head to the back of the bar where the dart boards are. I've never been great at darts, so it's no shock I'm losing. What *is* surprising, though, is how ridiculously good Bailey is—especially after claiming he doesn't play much.

"Damn, Bailey. Why don't you just take my money now?" I say after he hits his third bullseye.

We'd made a friendly wager—winner drinks for free the rest of the night, courtesy of the loser. Had I known

Bailey was a dart prodigy, I probably wouldn't have opened my mouth.

"I'm going to the bathroom, but when I get back, there's no stopping me," I joke, cracking my knuckles.

"I'm excited to see what kind of skills you cook up in there." Charlene laughs.

I give her a playful punch on the shoulder as I head off. Unsurprisingly, there's a long line for the ladies' room, and zero wait for the men's. At this point, my need to pee outweighs any sense of dignity, so I knock on the men's door.

Right as my fist goes to make contact with the wood for the third knock, the door swings open, and I'm face-to-face with the one person who's been avoiding me all night.

I blink at Liam, debating whether to say something or pretend we've never met. Against my better judgment, I go with the former.

"Hey. Um… the line's too long for the ladies', so I, uh…" I gesture awkwardly toward the bathroom behind him.

"Cool. I left the seat up for you," he says, brushing past me as he heads toward the table.

"Thanks, I—wait, what?" My brain stutters as his words register. I glance to my left and catch the girls at the front of the ladies' line giggling, flicking glances between me and Liam's retreating figure.

"It's not—he wasn't—ugh, never mind," I mutter, giving up on salvaging my pride. With a sigh, I walk into the men's bathroom and slam the door behind me.

What a prick.

I grab a wad of toilet paper and use it to lower the seat before handling my business.

When I return to the dart game, Bailey wipes the floor with Charlene and me in less than ten minutes. I take the loser's walk of shame to the bar to buy him a Sam Adams and a dirty martini for myself.

We rejoin the group at the table, fresh drinks in hand. Lindsey and Damon are back, too, with Lindsey smugly recounting her pool victory.

As I slide into my seat, I'm caught off guard when Liam actually speaks to me.

"How was the bathroom trip?" he asks, the corners of his mouth twitching into a smug smile.

Of course he'd say something like that.

"Go to hell," I shoot back, but I can't help the small snort of laughter that escapes me.

Liam turns to continue his conversation with Damon and slips right back into pretending I don't exist.

We don't speak for the rest of the night.

August 2024

If there's one more thing I've learned living in Salem, Massachusetts, for the past month, it's that Liam Doyle is a certified asshole. He has officially claimed the title of World-Class Jerk—with honors.

Ever since that first night at O'Neill's, we've barely spoken. But that doesn't mean I haven't seen him more than I'd like to. Anytime I hang out with Lindsey and her friends, he's there. Of course, he is. They've all known each other forever, and I—well, I basically parachuted into their lives out of nowhere. I try to remind myself of that when I feel annoyed that he's always invited. Still, I like to pretend I have the right to be bothered by his ever-present existence.

Most of the time, he acts like I'm invisible. But on the rare occasion he does acknowledge me, it's usually to do or say something borderline rude. Like last month, when we all met at Damon and Bailey's place for lunch, and he conveniently "forgot" my coffee order. One large hot vanilla latte. Not exactly rocket science. Or when he left me out of the group chat for Lindsey's birthday planning, and Charlene had to awkwardly add me afterward like a forgotten plus-one.

What really bothers me, though, is his smugness. He walks around like he's some enlightened woodland sage, better than the rest of us poor, unawakened souls, because he composts and practices moon rituals. And sure, on paper, he looks like a saint; he volunteers at the homeless shelter, cares about the environment, and even baked muffins for Lindsey last week when she was stressed about the looming school year. But none of that counts when he treats me like I'm some gum he has to scrape off the bottom of his ethically sourced boots.

Not that I've exactly turned the other cheek. I may have "accidentally" only ordered cheese pizzas for game night last weekend (he's lactose intolerant), and I might've quipped that he should see a witch doctor when he kept sneezing during a picnic we all had in Salem Commons. And okay, yes, maybe I refer to him as Satan or the Antichrist now and then. But only behind his back. That's just basic manners.

Even with the Antichrist in the mix, I still enjoy being around everyone else. They've welcomed me into their circle more than I expected, and I'm starting to feel like maybe I could belong. That thought is running laps in my head as I sit in the living room, waiting for Lindsey, who is currently breaking her own record for "Latest to Leave the House."

We were supposed to be out the door ten minutes ago. But I've known Lindsey long enough to know that punctuality is not one of her strong suits.

"Do you have an extra pair of sunglasses? I can't find mine!" she yells from her room.

I sigh and start to get up, prepared to dig through the abyss that is our shared junk drawer.

"Never mind! I found them!" she calls again before I've made it two steps.

"If we're not out the door in the next two minutes, they're going to leave without us, and we'll have to swim to catch up with them," I call back, calm but firm.

"Stop yelling at me! I'm almost ready!"

I arch a brow. "I don't think I'm the one who's yelling, but we might need a judge's ruling on that one," I mutter, mostly to myself, grabbing my beach bag and opening the front door.

Lindsey barrels down the hallway, sunglasses on and a White Claw already in hand. "See? I was ready. No need to shout. And it's my birthday—I'm allowed to be fashionably late." She taps my nose with her finger and breezes past me down the stairs.

"Again, I don't think I was the one who was—"

"Are you coming or what?" she calls.

I laugh and follow her into the thick, humid Salem air. Luckily, we live just a couple of blocks from the dock where everyone's meeting for the harbor excursion. When I first heard we'd be spending the day on a boat for Lindsey's twenty-ninth, I was excited. It's mid-August, and despite living minutes from the ocean, I haven't spent a single day by the water.

Then I found out it was *Liam's* boat. And my excitement took a nosedive.

It took some heavy convincing from Lindsey to get me to agree to spend an entire day afloat with a man who I'm fairly certain would toss me overboard if he thought he could get away with it. But she pulled the birthday card and promised not to leave me alone with him. That helped. A little.

Not that I would ever skip out on celebrating Lindsey. She deserves a party more than anyone. This morning, as a birthday gesture—and a *thank you for picking up the pieces of my life* gesture—I tried to cook Lindsey breakfast. Emphasis on *tried.* The eggs were too rubbery, the toast was basically charcoal, and the bacon set off the smoke alarm. She was sweet about it, though. Ate two bites, smiled, and offered to order bagels. That's friendship.

"There's the birthday girl! Finally," Damon calls as Lindsey and I step down the steep metal gangway onto the wooden public dock below. "We thought we were gonna have to set off without you."

"Oh please, you wouldn't dream of it," Lindsey says, playfully swatting his side.

He pulls her into a bear hug that looks like it might crush her. She's practically all limbs and sharp angles, and he's got enough muscle on him to make it seem like he might actually snap her in half.

"Okay, okay. My turn. Happy birthday, boo!" Charlene shouts, yanking Lindsey out of Damon's arms and into her own squeeze.

The other two guys step forward to give Lindsey their birthday wishes, each one offering a warm hug. I can't help but notice the way Bailey's hand lingers at the small of her back, his eyes fluttering shut just for a second as he pulls her in close and murmurs a happy birthday. Lindsey doesn't seem to be aware—she's already moving on to greet Liam—but I clock it. And it makes me smile a little.

I get hugs from everyone, too—minus Satan, of course. These people *really* like physical affection. I'm not used to that kind of friendship. My New York crew was more of the 'air kiss and eye roll' variety.

"Jenna! It's so good to see you again!" I exclaim, spotting the petite blonde beside Charlene and pulling her into a hug. Guess the hugging thing's rubbing off on me more than I thought.

Jenna's adorably tiny next to Charlene, who towers over both of us. Their height difference makes them even more charming as a couple. I've met Jenna a few times over the past weeks, and she's just as lovely and warm as Charlene.

"It's nice to see you, too! I was just saying to Char that—" Jenna begins to say, but is promptly cut off by none other than our fearless ship captain.

"All right, everyone ready? The launch is pulling in now," Liam barks, voice clipped.

We all answer with a collective "Yes!" and grab our stuff. I see the small motorboat that will ferry us to Liam's sailboat waiting at the end of the float.

"I guess witches don't learn patience in their practice," I whisper to Jenna and Charlene as we follow behind him, and they chuckle.

"I heard that, y'know," Liam calls over his shoulder without turning around.

"I meant for you to," I reply with a smirk.

He just shakes his head, annoyed but silent. I count that as a win.

As we make our way down the dock, we pass a group hauling gear from what looks like an early morning fishing trip. We climb into the launch, and Liam gives the driver the name and location of his boat. I find a seat, and—of course—I end up next to Satan. Again. I don't know how this keeps happening. Thankfully, it's a short ride.

But that doesn't stop him from opening his mouth.

"So, are you a natural blonde, or do you bleach it?"

I shoot him a glare. "It's real," I say, sweet as poison.

"Whatever you say," he mutters, turning his gaze to the water.

Before I can come up with a better comeback, he's already standing up as the launch pulls up alongside a much bigger sailboat.

The hull is painted a deep navy blue, and the deck is lined with beautiful chestnut wood. The mast towers above us, sails still tucked away, ready to catch the breeze. It's genuinely gorgeous, not that I'd ever say that out loud. Wouldn't want it going to Liam's head. His ego is already inflated enough.

I climb the ladder onto the deck, following Charlene to where she stows her bag in a cubby under a bench. Liam and Bailey start untying the sails while the rest of us gather near the bow, sitting in a half-circle on the curved benches.

The harbor stretches out in front of us, dotted with boats of all shapes and sizes. Sunlight dances off the water. Some spots are calm like glass, others are rippling with the breeze. It's one of those perfect summer days that feels like it belongs in a movie.

"Everyone ready to set sail?" Bailey calls, pulling on a line as the mainsail rises.

Liam follows behind, raising the smaller sail at the front.

"Oh, captain, my captain! Would you mind passing me a beer before we're anchors aweigh?" Damon shouts, saluting dramatically.

Liam rolls his eyes but tosses him a beer anyway.

Soon, the wind's in our hair, and the boat's picking up speed. Charlene hands out canned drinks, and we try to cheer for Lindsey's birthday, but the choppy water sends half our drinks sloshing onto the deck. We laugh anyway. Eventually, the boys steer us back toward the calmer waters of the harbor.

"So, Freya, anyone cute you've got your eye on since moving to Massachusetts?" Charlene asks, giving me a sly smile.

I laugh. "No, not really. Slim pickings."

"Ah, come on. No one at work?" she presses.

"Definitely not," I say with a chortle and dramatic shake of my head.

I started at *The Harbor Light* newspaper a month ago, and while my writing has never been better, I haven't exactly found my office bestie, let alone any eligible bachelors. Although I think I'm forever scarred from ever dating a coworker again. During lunch breaks, the other writers head out together while I'm left with my sad little container of leftover pasta. Just last week, I tried joining their conversation in the break room, commenting on the true-crime podcast they were raving about, but I mispronounced the host's name, and everyone went silent like I'd just insulted their grandmother.

"Well, maybe I'll have to set you up with someone soon," Charlene teases, a mischievous twinkle in her eye.

I don't know how else to end the conversation, so I just smile and say okay before I turn to Lindsey and change the subject.

"How are your parents doing on their trip to Vancouver? Are they sad to miss your birthday?"

"I think a little, but they're having the best time. And my grandma's loving having them all to herself. But they really want to see you when they get back!" Lindsey says.

"I can't wait! And I'm excited to finally see the house you grew up in," I reply.

"So you'd never visited Salem before moving here, Freya?" Bailey asks as he and Liam finally join us. I hadn't even noticed we'd stopped at the mouth of the harbor—the sails tucked away and the boat gently bobbing at anchor.

"No, never. I always wanted to, but in school, I couldn't afford to fly out. And after that, life just… got in the way," I say, a little embarrassed at the notion that I had never been to my best friend's childhood home when she had been to mine too many times to count. I feel even more guilty knowing that even though I personally couldn't have paid for a trip here during college, I always could have asked my parents for the funds, seeing as they have more than enough. But I hated doing that because their money always came with conditions. A hundred bucks in exchange for my attendance at an event my mom was hosting. Five hundred if I interned for a summer at my dad's firm. The higher the cost, the more strings attached.

"Hey, you made up for it when you dropped everything in New York to move here and be my roommate again," Lindsey says, pulling me into a side hug. I lean my head into the crook of her neck.

"If you don't mind me asking… why *did* you drop everything in New York to move here?" Damon asks, tentative. Charlene elbows him hard, and he yelps. "Ow! What? I'm just curious."

"It's okay, really," I say quickly. "I just… needed something different. Something a little more real. Plus, my family lived way too close to me," I finish with a laugh, trying my best to make half the truth sound convincing.

For some reason, my gaze goes to Liam to check if I succeeded. Our eyes meet for a fraction of a second before he averts his and looks down at his watch. I could tell he had been staring at me before I looked up at him.

"It's true. The Whitneys are *intense,*" Lindsey chimes in. "They're really high up in New York society because of Mr. Whitney's job, so they care a *lot* about image and class."

My cheeks burn. "You make it sound like we're Manhattan royalty," I say, trying not to sound defensive.

"You might as well be! I've seen your childhood home and the parties your parents host," Lindsey says with a laugh, not picking up on my hint for her to stop.

I laugh, trying to act like I'm not mortified. I know Lindsey's just showing her support for me, but I wasn't planning to air out all my family drama today. Her friends don't know me like she does yet. And I wanted them to before I shared about my upbringing.

However, from what I can tell, no one is looking at me with judgment or disgust, as I feared. No one seems to care that I'm the privileged girl with rich parents from the Upper East Side. Maybe none of that matters to them.

"Just because that's where you come from doesn't mean that's who you are, Freya," Charlene adds, her voice soft and sincere. She must have sensed my discomfort.

It was nice of her to say, although I didn't want to tell her that I was afraid she might not be right. What if we can never escape who we were raised to be?

"Thanks, Char. Anyway, who wants to jump in?" I say, desperate to shift the attention off me.

I tug off my T-shirt, revealing my red bikini top. Out of the corner of my eye, I see Liam quickly avert his gaze toward the mainland, but not before catching a glimpse.

"I do!" Jenna yells excitedly.

"Me too!" Lindsey adds.

"I'm in… but only if Bailey protects me from the sharks," Damon says, grinning at him. Bailey rolls his eyes but nods.

"I'll stay on board. Someone's gotta make sure the anchor doesn't slip," Liam says, settling in at the wheel and cracking a beer.

"Can't you just cast a spell to hold it in place?" I tease. It's just too easy.

He squints up at me. "You know that gap in your teeth makes you spit when you talk?"

Ouch. Okay, that one stung a little.

Eventually, we're all in the water, except Liam. I almost start to feel bad for him, sitting there alone. But then I remember how much of a jerk he's been since day one, and the sympathy vanishes. If he wanted to have a good time with his friends, then he could. Nothing is stopping him except his own inability to have fun.

Still, as I float in the water and glance back at the boat, I see him at the bow, beer in hand, a somber expression on his face.

And despite myself, despite *everything*—I feel a small, sharp pang in my chest.

***

When we finally get back to the mainland, everyone's sun-kissed and exhausted—except for Lindsey, who's still buzzing with energy like the human sparkler she is. We spent way more time out on the water than we originally planned. By the time we are all parting ways at the dock, we only have an hour before we need to meet back up for Lindsey's birthday dinner at Ledger's Restaurant.

Lindsey and I make it back to the apartment within ten minutes of getting off the launch. We shower, get ready, and by some miracle, we're the first to arrive. The host seats us at a long rectangular table in the back, Lindsey at the head, and me to her right.

Reservations were tough to get tonight, and now I see why. Every table is full, every corner buzzing. Ledger's is clearly a local hotspot. Lindsey mentioned it used to be a bank years ago. I can see remnants of that history from the grand architecture and high ceilings. The restaurant's interior pays homage to the building's roots with the large, open vault door leading to the kitchen and the old bank ledger books on a long, horizontal shelf above the bar.

Charlene and Jenna arrive within the next few minutes, followed by Damon and Bailey. Liam is the last to show up. Everyone settles in just as the server swings by to take our drink orders.

"I'll have a Cosmo, please. And it's my birthday today, so if there's anything you can do to make it extra special, that would be incredible," Lindsey says with a wink, absolutely shameless.

"Ignore her. She's just fishing for your number," Charlene quips from beside me. Our server, whose name tag reads *Matt*, chuckles. He is cute, I have to say.

"Well, I'll have to check in the back, but maybe I can make a few birthday wishes come true tonight," he flirts back, and Lindsey giggles.

"Don't mean to interrupt you two lovebirds, but I'll take a Budweiser," Damon says dryly. We all chime in with our orders, and Matt disappears to the bar.

As conversation bubbles up around the table, Charlene turns to me. "I love your sundress, Freya. Where'd you get it?"

"Thank you! Saks Fifth Ave. You can take the New Yorker out of New York, but you can't take New York out of her clothes," I quip, and we both giggle. "Your blouse is adorable too, where's that from?" I gesture to her pink top.

I don't even hear her response because I get distracted when Liam, who is sitting across from Charlene, rolls his eyes at me. I try to ignore him, but it's getting harder to do so. It's as if he thinks I'm lying, and I actually hate her top and her personality and everyone else in the group, and I'm just trying to leech onto them because I don't have any real friends of my own. Which, okay, fine, that last part might sting with some truth, but I genuinely like these people. I'm not just here because I have nowhere else to go.

Matt returns with our drinks and takes our meal orders, and then Lindsey claps her hands together. "Okay! Time for presents!"

She starts with Charlene and Jenna's gift—a gorgeous pearl necklace from a local jeweler. Then she opens Liam's: a set of four handmade candles, one for each season, from a witchy shop in town. It's a little cheesy, sure, but I can't deny they smell amazing, and Lindsey clearly loves them.

Next is Bailey's gift: a vinyl of *Heathers*, Lindsey's favorite musical, and a coupon for dinner for two at the Hawthorne Hotel.

"I figured you could use it for a date or something. Maybe you could take our waiter," Bailey says, half-joking, though the jealousy in his voice is barely masked. Lindsey, oblivious, thanks him and gives him a big hug.

"Okay, my turn!" Damon yells, tossing a poorly wrapped gift across the table. Lindsey miraculously catches it before it sends her Cosmo flying.

"It's nothing fancy," he says, "but I thought you'd appreciate it."

She unwraps it to reveal a pink T-shirt that reads *I have a musical theater degree and a full-time job... I can do anything* in bold letters. Lindsey cackles and proudly holds it up.

"Thanks, D! I'm wearing this to work every day from now on." She turns to me, beaming. "Okay, Freya. Last but not least."

"Don't get too excited. I'm definitely not topping the T-shirt." I reach under my chair for the small, wrapped gift.

"It's nothing huge. I figured we could also do something fun in Boston, but I wasn't sure what spots you liked best, so I didn't want to plan anything specific yet," I say as she opens the gift to reveal the book. "It's one of my recent favorites. I didn't see it around the apartment, so I figured you hadn't read it yet."

"I haven't! Thank you, I was actually in need of a new book." Lindsey squeezes my arm gratefully.

As she puts the book away, I hear Liam whisper something under his breath from across the table. He thinks I don't notice, but I do, and honestly, I'm tired of letting the rude comments slide.

"I'm sorry?" I say to him.

"Nothing. I just thought that maybe Lindsey's 'best friend' would have gotten her something a little more close to the heart for her birthday," He says, putting air quotes around the words best and friend. "You know she doesn't even like to read, right?"

"Hey! I do so like to read," Lindsey defends herself. But I'm still focused on the insult he threw my way.

"Well, at least I didn't get her some new age-y, whimsical, woo-woo crap that doesn't even fucking *do* anything," I snap back.

He presses his lips together, unbothered. "Real mature, Fiona."

"All right, who had the salmon?" Matt asks with a bubbly smile as he suddenly appears with our food, not realizing he's interrupting a heated conversation. I can't even focus on dinner anymore, though, not when Liam's smug face is egging me on from across the table.

"You *know* my name is Freya, you jackass," My voice raises to a louder volume, and everyone is visibly on edge to be witnessing yet another public outburst between Liam and I.

"Uhhh... why don't you come back in a few minutes?" Lindsey says to Matt, giving him a tight-lipped smile. He sends her a small nod before quickly leaving with the food to escape the rising tension at our table. I continue before Liam can cut in.

"You talk such a big game of being all 'peace and love' and 'salt of the earth.' But really, you're just a weird kid who was raised by weird people and doesn't want to admit that he's not normal." That probably stepped over the line more than the wolf comment did. For some reason, he makes me so angry, and I just can't help but say every mean thought that pops into my head. I think I struck a nerve, though, because Liam's face hardens, and he finally raises his voice to meet my level.

"My parents are good people, and they raised me right. That's more than I can say for yours. Judging by how stuck-up and conceited you are, I can only imagine what kind of nightmare they must be." His face is held in a stern expression, and his eyes are fully dilated, staring straight into mine.

I notice Damon chugging his beer while the girls look around the room awkwardly, pretending not to listen.

"At least I don't act like I'm the second coming of Jesus Christ, or whatever the equivalent of that would be for a witch." I'm not backing down, and neither is he.

Heads turn toward us from nearby tables as we shout even louder, and our fight escalates.

"Guys, maybe let's just—" Bailey starts, but Liam cuts him off.

"At least I'm not using Lindsey and all her friends as some makeshift distraction to escape whatever I'm running from. You just dropped into town and expected everyone to instantly fall in love with you. But you've been condescending since day one. And honestly? We're sick of pretending we want you here."

The tension in the room bursts, as if someone pricks the growing bubble of animosity with a needle. Then, there's a stillness after the devastation of the storm.

I'm so taken aback by his comment that I stare at him in silence for a few seconds, trying to formulate my comeback. But the truth is, I can't think of anything clever to say because that hit like a punch to the gut. Everything he said is exactly what I've been afraid of since I arrived. That they all secretly think I don't belong.

We're all left in dumbstricken silence, which no one dares to break until finally, I respond.

"If that's what you think, then fine. I'll leave."

I stand and grab my purse from the back of my chair.

"Freya. I didn't mean that," Liam begins to say, but I'm not listening anymore.

"I'm sorry, Lindsey. I'll see you at home," I say, trying to fight back tears.

She tries to stop me. So do Charlene and Jenna. But I'm done. I didn't come here to deal with someone like *him*. Arrogant, condescending, critical. He's exactly the kind of person I was trying to get away from when I left New York.

I push in my chair and turn to leave. But before I take a step, I pause and look back at the table, locking eyes with Liam.

"The book is a collection of biographies about female folk singers from the '60s. I got it for Lindsey because she loves that era of music, and I know she's always wanted to start writing her own songs. I thought it might give her some inspiration."

I glance at Lindsey. There's a small smile on her lips, though her eyes are tinged with sadness. Then I turn back to Liam.

"You can say a lot of things about me, but don't ever underestimate how much I care about that woman."

I don't wait for a response. I just turn and walk toward the door.

People watch me curiously as I pass, trying to piece together what just happened.

"Freya, wait!" Liam calls from behind me.

But it's too late.

I'm already gone.

Chapter 6

The morning after the disastrous birthday dinner, I wake up with a raging headache. And it's not from the booze.

When I got home last night, I cried myself to sleep watching reruns of *Friends* on my laptop and using my online shopping addiction as a coping mechanism. Now I'm down three hundred dollars with two Free People dresses arriving Tuesday. Shockingly, I still feel like shit.

I didn't hear Lindsey come in last night, but judging by the chaos coming from the kitchen, I know she made it home safely. All I want to do is spend the day in bed, watching rom-coms, and eating my weight in mac and cheese. But against my better judgment, I swing my legs over the edge of the mattress and get up.

As I walk down the hall, my phone buzzes in my hand. I glance down. It's my mom—again. I ignore it like I usually do. I probably should call her back soon, but I don't have the energy to argue with *anyone* else this weekend.

When I reach the living room, I stop short. My eyes land on a massive platter of assorted breakfast items sitting on the coffee table.

"Heyyyy…" Lindsey says cautiously, stepping out of the kitchen.

"What's all this?" I ask, gesturing toward the spread of croissants, muffins, and danishes.

"It's an apology brunch!" Charlene chimes in, appearing behind her.

"Oh. Hey, Charlene. I didn't know you were here," I say, caught off guard.

"We wanted to check in after last night," Jenna adds as she walks in behind Charlene.

"Oh wow, is *everyone* here this morning? Should I expect to find Bailey and Damon hiding in the bathroom?" I mutter, flopping down on the couch. I reach for what looks like an apple danish.

Lindsey laughs. "No, it's just us girls. We just wanted you to know that last night wasn't your fault. You had every right to be upset," she says, sitting beside me. The other two girls settle into the armchairs across from us.

"Yeah," Jenna says, "and nothing Liam said was true. We're really happy you moved here, and that we're becoming friends."

I sigh. "That means a lot, really. Thank you. I'm just not sure how much more I can take from Liam. I want to be your friend, but he's making it *really* difficult."

"We get it. We really do. But he *is* sorry. He said so right after you left," Charlene says eagerly. "He regrets everything that's happened and just wants to try and be friends."

"Forgive me if I don't exactly buy that," I reply, trying to keep my voice even. I do appreciate the effort, though. "I get that you guys want to defend him—he's your friend, and I respect that. But honestly? The only way I'm going to believe he actually wants to fix things is if I hear it directly from the horse's mouth."

Right on cue, there's a knock at the door.

I raise an eyebrow. I start to wonder who could possibly be here this early in the morning. But then I remember both Charlene and Jenna are currently sitting in my living room, so it's entirely possible that more of the 'fix it' crew are arriving now.

"And another thing," I add, standing as I head toward the door. "Even if the Antichrist himself showed up here begging for forgiveness, what makes you think I'd give it to him? Let's all just recap how he's treated me this past month and acknowledge that I'm *well within my right* to never speak to him again."

I swing open the front door, fully expecting Bailey with a tray of coffees or Damon with an "I'm sorry" fruit basket.

Instead, I come face-to-face with the last person I want to see this morning. Satan in the flesh.

"H–Hey," Liam stammers, meeting my eyes. "I just wanted to, uh—"

In my shock, I do the only thing I can think to do: I panic and slam the door in his face.

"Okay. Well, we're off to a *great* start here," Jenna says under her breath.

"Why didn't you tell me he was coming?!" I whisper-shout.

"We thought you wouldn't agree to see him," Lindsey says as if it's the most obvious thing in the world.

I laugh. Not because it's funny—because it's so *not* funny I might scream.

"Well, you thought right!" I yell. I can't help it. I'm furious—at Liam for having the audacity to show up here, at the girls for not telling me he was going to show up here, at myself for getting out of bed this morning.

"Listen, Freya… please just hear him out," Charlene says gently. "He's been through a lot this past year. And yeah, that's not an excuse for how he's treated you, but he's not a bad guy. You know Lindsey. You know *us* now, too. Do you really think we'd be close with someone who was actually like that all the time?"

I guess I do have to agree with that last part. But I ignore the bit about how he's been through a lot this year. Because she's right, it doesn't excuse anything. I've been through a lot, too. You don't see me going around being a jerk to everyone I meet.

"Plus," Lindsey adds, "it's not like *you've* been super accepting of him either. I'm not saying you started it, but… you haven't exactly tried to fix it, either. You can be kind of rigid when it comes to people who don't fit the mold. And Liam? He's basically mold-proof. Maybe what you two need is a little one-on-one time to actually understand each other."

"Hey, I *did* try! At the beginning, at least…" I trail off, then sigh. "Okay. Okay, you've got a point."

My mind drifts to all the snarky things I've said to him over the last month. I mean… calling someone the Antichrist behind their back doesn't exactly scream innocence.

The New Yorker in me wants to shout, "He thinks he's a witch!" in my defense. But I know that kind of thinking doesn't fly here. I'm not surrounded by Upper East Side socialites anymore. These people—they're better. And if I want to be friends with them, I need to be better too.

Another knock.

"Freya, please. I just want to talk," Liam says quietly through the door.

All three girls look at me, faces full of hopeful expectations.

I exhale slowly. He *does* sound sincere.

I glance down at my feet, then back toward the door. Against my better judgment—and possibly my sanity—I turn the knob.

As the door opens again, I really look at him this time. His hair is a mess, not in its usual artful shag. There are dark circles under his eyes, a sure sign he didn't sleep last night. His hands are shoved in his pockets, and when he looks at me, there's something raw and pleading in his expression.

Those eyes. *God*, those green eyes.

"Do you want to… go for a walk or something?" he asks, uncertain.

"Fine," I say, voice firm. "But a short one."

Relief flashes across his face.

"Let me get changed quickly," I add before retreating to my room. I close the door behind me, lean against it, and take a deep breath.

This walk could either fix everything… or make it a hell of a lot worse.

And I can't tell which one I'm hoping for.

***

It's another perfect summer day. The sun blazes down onto the pavement as Liam and I walk in complete silence. Awkward silence. Fearful silence, even. I don't want to be the first to speak. And I don't think he does either. We pass under the tall metal gates of Salem Commons, right in front of The Witch Museum, when Liam finally speaks.

"Nice day out," he says.

I scoff and roll my eyes.

"What?" he asks, already defensive.

"'Nice day out'? Really? That's all you have to say to me right now? Y'know, the girls talked you up a lot, but I knew this was going to happen. You have no idea how to apologize, and honestly? I don't think this is worth it. I'm just going to go back home." I turn and start to walk away.

"Wait—Freya…" he starts, but I don't listen.

"Stop!" he shouts.

Something in his voice makes me freeze, though I don't turn around. He's quiet for a second before continuing.

"I'm trying, okay? This is me trying not to be such an asshole."

At that, I turn. We're a few paces apart, but I finally look at him.

"I'm sorry. Truly. I'm sorry for everything. I'm sorry I embarrassed you in front of the tour group when we first met. I'm sorry I called you ignorant for not believing in what I believe. That wasn't fair—you were just expressing your opinion. I see that now."

He takes a few steps closer, his voice softer.

"And I'm so, *so* sorry for what I said last night. I didn't mean it. I've been a total dick to you this past month. I let my anger—anger that had nothing to do with you—control how I acted, and that's not okay. You didn't deserve any of it." He hesitates. "Well, most of it. I just… I care a lot about how I was raised and my roots in Salem. Sometimes, I get overly defensive when I feel like people are criticizing that."

I watch him closely, trying to decide whether or not I believe him. But honestly? I could tell from the moment he started speaking, he means it.

"I forgive you," I say, my voice soft. I want this feud to end just as much as he does. Maybe even more.

"…Okay," he says, bobbing his head slightly. He finally breaks eye contact and looks down at his shoes.

"Will you do something for me?" I ask after a beat.

He looks up again and nods slowly.

"Will you just… explain all of this to me? Because I've felt kind of lost ever since moving here," I say, gesturing vaguely toward The Witch Museum. He looks confused.

"…You want me to explain the Salem Witch Trials to you?"

"Well, yeah. That—and how that history shaped the town and how *you* grew up. I guess I just don't get how a tragedy from over three hundred years ago still affects a place and its people so deeply. To me, it just seems like people are profiting off a tragic past. With all the shops, museums, psychics, ghost tours…" I trail off, realizing I may have offended him. "Not that *you're* trying to do that!"

To my relief, he lets out a chuckle.

"But seriously, doesn't it ever make you wonder who's really here because they care about the history, and who's just here to make a cheap buck?" I ask. Saying it out loud is oddly freeing—I hadn't voiced this to anyone yet.

Liam nods, understanding flickers across his face. "I can see how it'd be hard to understand if you didn't grow up with the stories and the historical reminders around every corner."

He pauses, then turns and starts toward the crosswalk.

"Come on. I want to show you something," he calls over his shoulder.

I follow him as he crosses the street, expecting him to lead me into the museum. But instead, he veers down a narrow road beside it. After a few minutes, we reach a small, rectangular green space next to an old cemetery. It's maybe ten yards long and five wide, bordered by granite walls on three sides and dotted with locust trees in the middle.

Walking paths frame the grassy area, and lining each path are stone benches mounted directly into the walls.

"Where are we?" I ask, looking around.

"This is the Salem Witch Trials Memorial," he says as he starts to walk up the path on the right.

At first, I'm confused. There's no statue or plaque, nothing like a traditional memorial. But then I notice the stone benches. Each has a name and a date carved into the top.

"Everyone who was executed during the trials has a bench in their memory. It's not much, but it's quiet. Simple. And I think people appreciate that there's a space that pays tribute to the victims. I know I do."

I follow behind him, reading each name as we pass.

"How many people died?" I ask quietly, not wanting to disturb the peace.

"At least twenty-five. The twenty who were executed have benches here, but others died in jail waiting for trial," Liam says. "It wasn't like Europe, where thousands died, but for here, it was significant—especially since it happened right after the colonies were settled. And a lot more people were accused, too. They were only freed when the governor stopped the court from going forward with any more trials after his own wife was accused of witchcraft."

"Wow. I didn't even know that's how it ended," I murmur, mostly to myself.

"People who don't understand the trials brush it off as a minor, inconsequential event. But it wasn't. Not for Salem. Its effects lingered for centuries, especially since the victims and their families never got true justice. Did you know Massachusetts didn't officially apologize until 1957? That's over two hundred years after everyone involved was already dead."

I stare at him in disbelief. "No, I had no idea."

He nods solemnly as we round the loop at the top and turn down the other side.

"Salem's past has been scrutinized for years, always viewed as a dark mark left on the city. It's hard to reconcile an event as tragic and inhumane as the Witch Trials. But more recently, people have tried to bring those stories into the light—not to glorify them, but to make sure they're never forgotten. That's why some people here still celebrate Pagan religions and practice witchcraft. It's a way to remember the ones who were lost."

"But… I thought the people who were executed weren't actually witches," I say, confused.

"They weren't."

Now I'm even more confused. "Then why commemorate them with the very thing that caused them to lose their lives in the first place?"

He takes a moment before answering. "None of the victims were witches. But when they were accused of *being* witches, they were met with fear, hate, and intolerance. Modern Pagan and Wiccan communities are based upon the principles of acceptance and social justice. So, they've rooted their communities here in defiance of the way the government persecuted people who didn't deserve it. People who they declared to be different, and therefore wrong.

"They're saying: we remember. And we stand for what those victims *should* have been given—respect, freedom, and dignity."

I can hear the passion in his voice, and for the first time, I actually understand where he's coming from.

"Huh. I guess that makes sense," I say, surprised to find myself agreeing with Liam about witchcraft, of all things. He chuckles and rolls his eyes, sitting on one of the benches at the end of the path, leaving a space for me.

Before I sit, I glance down at the name.

"Bridget Bishop. You mentioned her on your tour—the first to be executed."

"Mm-hmm. I like her bench the best. Actually, she's my ancestor, on my mom's side," he says, giving me a small smile as I settle down next to him.

"Really?" I'm surprised he can trace his lineage back that far. Then again, he did say his family had been here since the town was first settled.

"Yep. Distant relative. Her children stayed in Salem after she was executed, and some never left. So… here I am." He shrugs his shoulders.

"That's incredible. I didn't realize your roots here ran that deep."

We sit in silence, listening to the birds chirping and the breeze rustling through the trees.

"Thank you for sharing all of this with me. I feel like I actually… understand a little more now," I say sincerely.

"Anytime. I *am* somewhat of a history buff, in case you hadn't noticed. I'm always happy to spew out all kinds of stories from the past. As long as you've got a couple hours to spare once you get me going."

I laugh. That might be the first time he's ever made a joke with me. He's funny, in his own nerdy way.

"I'm sorry, too," I say after a quiet moment. "I've been acting like a child since the night we met, and I've said a lot of things I didn't mean. I've been petty. I was so angry with you after that first night, and… sometimes it's hard for me to let go of things when someone hurts me."

"I get it. I hold grudges, too," he says as if that wasn't already obvious. I laugh again before continuing.

"I made a snap judgment—about you, and about Salem. And I'm sorry for that. You may not be *completely* unhinged after all."

"Oh, thank God. Only *mildly* unhinged, then?" he says with a grin.

We sit there in silence for another moment before he speaks again.

"Would you like to get some coffee?"

Chapter 7

The Red Line Café on Essex Street is bustling with the Sunday morning rush. Some hurry through the line to order a coffee to-go and leave as quickly as they came. While others bask in a leisurely morning with a friend, chatting at one of the round wood tables near the windows.

In combination, the smell of roasted coffee beans mixed with the warm yellow lighting, the large cushy arm chairs, and the smooth jazz playing low from a small speaker create a cozy and pleasant ambience in the room.

"Go grab that table in the corner before it gets taken. I'll get us some coffee," Liam says as we step inside and join the long line.

"Okay. I think I have some cash that I can—" I begin, rummaging through my purse for my wallet.

"It's all good. My treat," he says casually. "A peace offering for being such an ass."

I chuckle and thank him, starting toward the free table in the back. But I stop mid-step, spinning around when I realize I never told him my order.

"Oh! Can I get a lar—"

"Large hot vanilla latte. I remember. Now go grab that table. It's getting crowded in here," he says, gesturing toward the big group that just walked in.

A small flutter stirs in my stomach. He remembers my order from three weeks ago? I knew he was lying when he said he forgot. A smile creeps onto my face as I make my way to the open table. I slide onto the bench and place my purse in the chair opposite me to save the seat for Liam.

A few minutes later, he returns with two steaming mugs in hand. He sets one in front of me, then moves my purse to the bench beside me before sitting down. I take a sip of my latte and glance around the café.

"So, you really don't find any of this even the slightest bit cheesy?" I ask, nodding toward a mural of a green witch flying on a broomstick.

He twists to look at the painting behind him, then raises his hands in mock surrender. "All right, sure. Some of it gets a little overboard. I admit it."

I smirk, feeling a small flicker of triumph. Just a flicker, though.

"Obviously, Salem's become a huge tourist town, so there's a surface layer of gimmicks and smokescreens, especially during October. I hope you're ready for that, by the way," he says, raising an eyebrow. "But if you know where to look and what to avoid, you'll find most of the culture here is rooted in authenticity, not scams."

He lifts his mug to his lips.

"You'll have to help me with that," I say. "I have a terrible habit of trusting things that look shiny and well-branded."

"I'm always here to help," he responds with a small smile.

I return the smile and take another sip. "Tell me about your childhood here."

He pauses for a moment, a thoughtful expression on his face. I'm realizing how much I like hearing him talk.

"Well, I'm an only child. I grew up with my mom and dad in a house overlooking the ocean. We've always been close. I don't really have an extended family, just my mom's sister and her husband. They helped raise me. But they never had kids, so I was always the only one around, which, honestly, I loved. I got all the attention." He flashes a cheeky grin.

I giggle.

"My dad grew up in Ireland. He came here after finishing school. And my mom was born here. Both of them are Wiccan. My mom and aunt were raised in the religion by their mother, who was one of the original practitioners in the sixties. And my dad started practicing when he met my mom. She taught him everything. Then, when I came along, they passed it all on to me."

"You've mentioned that before. What, uh… what exactly is it?" I ask, hesitating, unsure if I'm wording it right.

"Wicca?" he says.

"Mm-hmm. Lindsey said you were a witch, but I figured there's more to it."

He chuckles. "It's a newer form of Paganism—which is basically a term for pre-Christian religions. It's a modern way of practicing witchcraft. A way to understand it in today's world."

"Huh. So… you *are* a witch?" I ask cautiously.

"Sort of. But not in the way you're picturing."

"You don't wear a pointy hat and fly around on a broomstick?"

He rolls his eyes. "No. And we don't worship the devil. We worship nature. Mother Earth. We believe in the energy of the universe and in the spirits of those who've passed—and how they still affect the world around us."

"Oh. So, do you go to a church or something like that?"

"Not really. That's what I love most about Wicca, it's flexible. Most people practice on their own, however they want. There's no central dogma. No one-size-fits-all belief system. As long as you 'do no harm,' you're free to follow your own path. We also celebrate a lot of Pagan holidays, like the solstices and equinoxes, among others."

Even though I've never heard of half the things he's talking about, I still feel like I understand him.

"Really, it's all about the belief that positive thinking brings about positive change. My mom always says witchcraft, at its core, is about kindness—to others, to the planet, and to yourself. She thinks if more people understood it, maybe they'd treat each other a little better."

He looks thoughtful for a beat, like he's wandered somewhere deep, and I suddenly feel like I've stumbled into something private.

"She sounds like a lovely person," I say softly.

He smiles. "She is."

"I think I'm understanding it all. Or at least more than I did before," I say with a shrug.

"Baby steps," he says.

I chuckle. "Man. I feel like we didn't even grow up on the same planet. My parents have never said anything that profound to me in my entire life. Are you sure it's even legal for you to be talking to me right now?"

He laughs. "I bet we've got more in common than you think."

"I highly doubt it. But give it your best shot," I say, teasing.

He leans back and pretends to think hard. "Hmm… do you like music?"

"I think everyone likes music."

"Favorite genre?"

"Rock. Or country, depending on the time of year."

"Favorite artist?"

"Green Day. Definitely."

"Huh. I'm more of a Blink-182 guy, but I'll accept your answer," he says, grinning in a way I haven't seen before. I like that smile. I hope I get to see it again.

"I wouldn't have pegged you for a rock fan."

"What, were you expecting bubblegum pop?" I joke.

"Well… yeah. Pretty much," he says with a shrug.

I laugh. "My brother was really into punk rock growing up. I guess it just stuck with me. I think the fact that my parents hated the stuff made me like it that much more."

He laughs, then goes quiet. For a few seconds, he just looks at me.

"Tell me something else about you," he finally says.

I think for a moment. "I love old movies."

"What's your favorite?"

"Well, that's tricky… but I'd probably have to go with *It's a Wonderful Life*. I used to watch it with my family every Christmas when I was a kid. It's a rare fond memory I have from childhood."

His eyes widen slightly, and he shoots me a dubious look. "No way," he says, suspicion thick in his voice.

"Don't act too surprised. I'm allowed to have good taste in films and music, y'know," I say, a little defensively.

Liam keeps staring at me, and it's starting to weird me out. Until, without a word, he pulls up the sleeve of his T-shirt and turns his shoulder toward me. I know what he's showing me before he even points.

Ink nestled among the other artwork on his arm: a full moon with a rope looped around it, the words *lasso the moon* written beneath. Just like the drawing Mary makes for George in the movie.

"It was one of the first ones I ever got," he says, glancing down at it with quiet fondness.

I can't help but reach out and trace the black lines gently with my fingertip. "It's beautiful. I can't believe you have that. I seriously love that movie."

"See? We do have something in common. My family watches it every year at Christmas, too."

My brows knit. "Wait… so, you celebrate Christmas?"

He exhales a small laugh and shakes his head. "Yes. And Yule, during that time of the year as well."

"I just assumed you wouldn't since you're… uh—"

"Wiccan?"

"Yes. Wiccan."

I brace myself for backlash, like what happened at O'Neill's last month. But instead, he just nods and takes a sip of his coffee before answering.

"Well, we do. Always have. My dad grew up Catholic, and he never wanted to give up the holiday. But y'know, a lot of the traditions associated with Christmas actually originated from Pagan beliefs."

"Really? Like what?" I ask, genuinely curious now.

"The Christmas tree, for one. Pagans would bring fir trees indoors during Yuletide to represent life and fertility. They'd decorate them with candles and ornaments to celebrate the sun's return after the Winter Solstice. And the Druids in Britain used mistletoe as a charm against evil and in fertility rites.

"Same with the Yule log, mulled wine, exchanging gifts, gathering with family—it all traces back to some version of Paganism."

"Seriously? I never knew that." I blink, realizing just how much I don't know.

"Yeah, well…" he mutters, rolling his eyes slightly.

The gesture hits me harder than I expect.

"Could you do me a favor?" I ask. "Maybe… don't react that way when I'm still trying to figure this stuff out? I'm not trying to be ignorant, I just want to understand."

He meets my eyes. We hold the gaze for a moment before he looks down, nodding.

"You're right. I'm sorry. I shouldn't put you down just because you grew up differently. That's not fair. I can tell you're trying, and I really do appreciate it."

"It's okay," I say. "I just figure, if I'm going to live here, I should probably try to learn. Especially since it looks like we'll be spending a lot of time together."

Liam nods. "You're right. And I'm glad you want to learn. I'm also glad you're not totally repulsed by the idea of having to hang out with me."

"Baby steps," I tease.

He smiles, then circles us back. "So, you celebrate Christmas. Were you raised Christian?"

"No. We didn't grow up practicing any religion. We were more of the culturally Christian type of family, I guess. Pretty sure both my parents are atheists, actually. We never went to church or anything. They're both so cynical about everything—religion, people, the world in general. I'm not sure they really believe in anything."

"Not even a higher power?" he asks.

"No. Unless you're talking about the power of money. Then they are devout worshippers," I joke lightly, but there's a bitter edge to it.

He chuckles along with me, but I can tell he notices the undercurrent.

"It was just tough growing up around people who didn't really believe in *me* either. I think I always felt like I had to prove myself. To earn my spot at the table somehow. And even when I did everything right, it still wasn't enough. It's like… I didn't come out the way they wanted." As I start talking, I can't seem to stop.

"It never felt like I fit into the family blueprint. My siblings? They fit. They became exactly who my parents wanted them to be. Meanwhile, everything about me just seemed to confuse them. They didn't know what to do with me. They didn't say it out loud, but I could feel it. Every decision I made, every dream I had—it just felt like more proof to them that I didn't belong. I went to Columbia when they wanted Harvard. I chose journalism when they expected law school." I let out a lifeless chuckle. "Moving here probably felt like just one more failure to them. Another thing they could shake their heads about."

I pause and then add, "Anyway, sorry. I'm ranting."

I've never been good at keeping my emotions inside for very long. I always try to keep everything locked in until, eventually, I start to overflow, and it all uncontrollably pours out to the first person who will listen. Before I know it, my whole life is laid out for someone to view on a small café table.

"No, no. Don't apologize. I feel like I'm finally understanding what makes you tick," he says. A small smile creeps onto my face. I feel the same way about him, but I don't voice that thought out loud.

"There's not much else beyond that. I moved out as soon as I left for college because I needed space to figure out who I was, not who they thought I should be. I wanted to prove that I could survive without them." I take a breath and then continue, "It's not that I don't appreciate some of the things they gave me—they provided for me, gave me opportunities. But it always felt like their love was conditional. And sometimes, I just need a break from feeling like I'm being weighed and measured all the time." I pause and take a sip from my coffee.

"That's really tough. I'm so sorry you have to deal with that," he says with genuine empathy. There's something about him that is so easy to talk to. And I just keep going.

"Honestly, my biggest fear is that even though I feel so different from them, I think I'm a little too much like them sometimes. Skeptical. Judgmental. Hard to please. And I hate that. I hate the idea that I'm carrying around the parts of them I tried so hard to get away from." I laugh a little under my breath, realizing how messy and tangled my thoughts sound.

"I don't think you're any of those things," Liam says after a few seconds of silence.

"Really? I'm honestly surprised to hear you say that. I've been horrible to you," I reply candidly.

He chuckles a bit. "Maybe I wouldn't have said that a month ago. But after today… I don't know. You're becoming a whole new person to me. Someone who, deep down, is actually the complete opposite of everything you're afraid you are."

My gaze drops to my lap for a moment as I think through his words. And then I smile a little to myself. I realize then that maybe what Charlene said on the boat was right. Maybe where I come from doesn't need to matter that much.

"I feel like I'm painting a really awful picture of my family right now. I don't mean to imply they're terrible people. Despite all of that, I do have some good memories as well." I add quickly, regretting a few of the things I've shared.

Liam shakes his head. "Families are complicated. And it's okay to rant about them. Healthy even. Believe me, I do it too. Doesn't mean you don't love them. And, judging from your circumstances, I think you're more than entitled to let the rant gates open every now and then." He adds, trying to comfort me further.

"Thanks. I try not to put that burden on friends too often, though. I used to do that in New York, and I think a lot of them got sick of hearing about it."

I still feel like I'm divulging too much information. But Liam doesn't seem to mind. He's listening intently and looks as if he wants to hear more. I know that I should cut myself off, though, before I'm lying down on the café bench spewing out every one of my childhood traumas while he jots his thoughts down on a yellow legal pad.

"So, are you saying… we're becoming friends now?" he asks, looking deep into my eyes. His green orbs are almost too hypnotizing.

"Yeah. Yeah, I guess we are," I agree. Friends. I like that.

Chapter 8

September 2024

If there are two things I've learned in almost three months of living in Salem, Massachusetts, it's that Liam Doyle isn't as much of an asshole as I thought he was—and I still have so much more to learn.

It's fall now. The hot summer sun has simmered down to a cool autumn glow, and all the trees have started to turn vibrant shades of orange and red. Fall is my favorite season. Autumn in Manhattan is hard to beat, and I was doubtful it would feel the same in Salem, especially with more witch paraphernalia coming to life as Halloween approaches. But now that I'm experiencing a real New England autumn, I'm realizing it may be even more beautiful than what I'm used to in the city. And the witches don't bother me as much as I thought they would. It's like the whole world is shifting in a way that feels fresh and promising.

Work is starting to feel the same way. I've fallen into a calming rhythm, which is a welcome change from the chaos I used to feel at my old job. My days have settled into a predictable flow: the smell of coffee beans roasting in the pot, the hum of endless chains of emails, and the click of the keys under my fingertips as I type up a good story. My coworkers no longer feel like strangers. And I no longer feel like the new girl. The little victories, like being asked for my input during meetings or receiving a warm smile when I walk into the office, make me feel like I'm finally fitting in. I even get invited out to lunch now.

The best thing about the change of season, though, is the fact that Liam and I have now completely moved out of the 'enemy' category and into the 'friend' one. I won't lie; it definitely took us a little while to find our footing. When you build a relationship with someone on curt insults, cheap tricks, and often pretending like the other person doesn't exist, it takes some getting used to when that same person starts being nice to you. Or when you actually *want* to be nice to them. We were the blind leading the blind at first, but we figured it out after about a week or two.

I was especially proud of myself when I didn't roll my eyes or make a snap judgment when Liam told us he was celebrating the Fall Equinox with his family this past week. I'm taking a page from the Pagans by practicing tolerance toward things I don't quite understand. It's a whole new me.

Somehow, Liam and I have turned Sunday morning coffee into a weekly ritual. It started out as an accident. The Sunday after our initial apologies, coffee, and truce, I bumped into him in line at the same café. What can I say? They make a really mean latte. He asked if I wanted to sit and chat for a bit, and that's exactly what we did. The next Sunday, he invited me again. And then again the next week. Now we're six Sundays in, and I don't see us stopping any time soon.

At first, I only agreed to meet him because Lindsey thought it would be good for us to continue to get to know each other better and 'solidify our friendship.' But somewhere between hating him and tolerating his presence, I actually started to enjoy his company. Now, I find myself rushing through the week just to get to Sunday.

Lindsey keeps referring to them as dates, and every time she does, I consider sending her an invoice for emotional damages.

Even if I did like Liam like that—which I absolutely, without a doubt, do NOT—dating is out of the question for me right now. I'm focused on work and building my new life in Salem. Since when did our society start placing such a high priority on finding love? I'm happy with my life as it is. At least, that's what I told Lindsey, and she responded with a smirk, a little shrug, and a cute "We'll see!" I swear, one day, I'm cashing in and buying myself a spa weekend.

Lindsey isn't the only one trying to get me out on a date. Charlene has tried to set me up three times now. I'm running out of ways to tell her "Thank you, but no. And please stop trying." At least she isn't suggesting I go out with Liam, though.

"Do we really have to do this?" I ask, almost whining.

"Yes. We do. You said you wanted to learn, and I'm trying to teach you, but there's only so much wisdom I can bestow unto you myself." Liam grins over his shoulder as he drags me inside. The museum doesn't look open yet, but somehow, we get in.

"Yes, but I thought we were going to skip the cheesy parts," I say a little too loudly as we pass the people at the welcome desk. I smile quickly, hoping they don't think I'm rude.

"This isn't cheesy. I promise," he replies, leading me to the ticketing window and finally dropping my hand. The slight electricity I felt rushing through my body vanishes immediately once the contact is broken.

"Hey, Jim. How are you?"

The older man behind the ticket window looks up at the mention of his name. His face immediately brightens when he sees us.

"Liam! So good to see you again. Let me come give you a proper greeting." Jim holds up his finger, signaling that he'll be right out. A few seconds later, he pushes through a hidden door to the left of the window and wraps Liam up in a big hug. Jim looks to be in his mid to late sixties—tall like Liam but with a much rounder belly and a bushy gray beard that complements his full head of gray hair.

"Oh, it's been too long! How have the tours been going?" Jim asks, still not letting Liam out of their embrace. When he catches a glimpse of me for the first time, he lets go of Liam's shoulders to gesture in my direction. "And who might this lovely lady be?"

I smile and go to introduce myself, but Liam beats me to it.

"This is my friend, Freya. She just moved to Salem a few months ago, and I've been slowly showing her around the city. I thought she was finally in need of a visit to the museum." Liam says, giving me a quick wink.

"Ah, well, it's nice to meet you, Freya! My name's Jim, and I'm the manager of The Witch Museum," Jim says as he extends his hand. I take it with a smile.

"It's great to meet you as well, Jim!" I grin up at him.

"You've come with the right person. Now that it's the end of September, the lines are starting to get pretty lengthy. Since Liam's a Salem tour guide, he has the perk of being able to slip in during our off hours." Jim grins.

"Oh, okay. At first, I thought we might have been breaking and entering just for the sake of history." I tease.

"Well, I can't think of a better reason to commit a felony." Jim laughs loudly. "I'll get you two started in the first room. Liam, I think you know the tour well enough to walk through without a guide?"

"I believe we're in the clear with that one." Liam chuckles.

"Well, you kids have fun. We open in an hour, so try to be out before then if you can." Jim opens one of the doors and motions us inside.

"No promises," Liam teases. I'm starting to see this side of him more and more—the jokester who doesn't take life too seriously. It's a refreshing change after the grumpy guy I was stuck with for the first month of knowing him.

We enter the large room, and Liam leads the way to a bench along the walls. The room is set up to hold a lot more people, but today, it's just us. Mannequins around the room depict different scenes from the Salem Witch Trials: a courtroom with a young girl testifying, a woman in a jail cell, a man being buried alive, and even one of the Devil himself. Some of the images are pretty gruesome, and I can't look at them for long.

Before I can ask about the scenes, the lights suddenly dim. The room falls into thick darkness, and then a voice begins narrating the story of how the Salem Witch Trials began, walking us through the timeline of events that led to the deaths of all the innocent victims. Each part of the narration is paired with one of the scenes, which lights up as the voice refers to them. There are voice actors who play pivotal roles in the story, like the girls who first accused their family's slave, Tituba, of witchcraft, which set off the hysteria. And Giles Corey, the man who was pressed to death by stones because he refused to stand trial.

By the time the lights come back on, I'm wiping tears from my cheeks.

"Are you okay?" Liam asks when he notices. I sniffle and offer him a small smile.

"I'm fine. Sorry, I just… I never knew." I'm still at a loss for words. "I was never taught any of this in school. And I guess I never thought to research it on my own, either. It's quite a sad story, really." I realize I'm stating the obvious, but I am still a little shocked by some of the details.

"It is. It's okay to feel a little dumbstruck by it. I don't think it's taught in much depth outside of Massachusetts. I mean, why would it be? For most places, it's just a small piece of American history. But here, it's something bigger."

As Liam finishes his thought, I realize his hand is rubbing small circles on my back. I don't know how long it's been there, and honestly, I don't think he realizes he's doing it, either. That is until I clear my throat and straighten up a little. The touch disappears as quickly as it came.

"All right, uh—now we continue this way." Liam stands up, looking a little awkward, and motions to an open door across the room leading to another hallway.

I stand and follow him through the exhibit, feeling a faint flush on my cheeks.

The next few displays share more about some other parts of the history of the trials and Salem's relationship to witchcraft in general. More mannequins act out scenes in display cases, and Liam rattles off different facts, historical tidbits, and personal anecdotes as we slowly walk through the halls. I find it all much more fascinating than I thought I was going to.

Toward the end of the tour, there are two cases sitting side by side. One shows a witch with a green face on her broomstick, wearing black robes and a pointy hat. A black cat sits on the broom with her as her companion. She looks as though she's letting out an evil cackle as she flies over the small village below her, the moon full in the distance.

The second case next to it shows two mannequins, a man and a woman, standing in the sunlit woods, dressed in somewhat modern clothes, and both wearing simple yet colorful cloaks. The plaques on the two cases explain the difference between witches in popular culture and modern witches who actually practice the Craft today. It's a lot like how Liam explained the difference to me last month at the café.

"Hey, look! They're Wiccans too. Do you know them?" I tease a bit, pointing at the display of the man and woman in the woods.

"Hmm… nope. Can't say that I do." Liam laughs, walking over to stand next to me and peer at the display.

As I continue to read the plaque explaining what the Wiccan religion is all about, I start to get confused again. I felt like I had a handle on it when Liam explained it to me, but this description is twisting up everything I thought I knew.

"So, it says here that Wiccans do actual magic in their practice? Like through rituals and stuff?"

"Yep. That's part of it. My family does rituals together all the time, or you can do them solo if you prefer. There aren't really any rules. As long as you do no harm to others." He shrugs casually.

"Now, this is what I don't understand. I get people want to celebrate Pagan holidays and carry on certain traditions and beliefs, but… there's no such thing as magic," I say matter-of-factly. "How can that be a part of a religion?"

Liam chuckles a little. "This is where you're getting confused. When we say 'Magick,' we don't mean the magic you're thinking of. Not like *Harry Potter* or *Sabrina The Teenage Witch*. In Paganism, Magick, spelled with a 'k' at the end, like this"—he points to the word spelled out in the blurb on the plaque—"can be anything you do or think that helps you achieve a desired change in your life. There are unseen forces, energy all around us. We're all made of that energy. Everything in the world is. Including our thoughts," he explains, but I'm still lost.

"What does that have to do with *Magick*?" I ask, putting air quotes around the word.

"Well, for example, when we do a ritual that's meant to bring us good fortune or protect our house from bad energy, the most important part of that ritual is our mindset. We have to actually believe our good intentions are going to come to fruition. That way, the energy of our thoughts manipulates the energy of the physical world. Eventually, the thing we prayed for—or manifested, or wished upon, however you want to phrase it—actually comes true.

"We might light candles, use certain herbs, pray to a deity, or repeat a specific phrase to help us get into a meditative state. But it's the mind that does the heavy lifting. If we can't visualize what we want, then it won't come true."

Liam finishes, and I stand there silently for a moment, trying to digest what he just explained.

"I know it can be tricky to understand. And really, that's just the tip of the iceberg, but I don't want to overwhelm you with a bunch of new age, metaphysical jargon you're just going to think is stupid," he says, looking a little dejected.

"No, no! I don't think it's stupid. Sorry, I just—it's a lot of information to absorb, but I think I get it. It's like quantum physics," I say, realizing I actually do comprehend what he's talking about.

He chuckles. "Yes, exactly. Leave it to you to equate Magick with science," he says, shaking his head with a small smirk.

"Well, now that you've explained it like that, I actually understand it way more. We're all made up of the same energy. And like attracts like. So, when you think positive thoughts, positive things will be brought into your life?" I ask, checking if I'm understanding him right.

"Mm-hmm. It's like karma. And negative thoughts will bring about negative energy, too," he says. "You can think of it in any way you want, but in the tradition I was raised in, when you're focusing your mind like that with intention, technically… you're practicing witchcraft." Liam starts walking toward the exit.

"Whoa. So *I* could be a witch?" I ask hesitantly, and he laughs.

"Yeah. You can join the club. We need more people like you. The skeptics keep us on our toes."

I chuckle and follow him out of the room. Maybe someday soon, I should give this whole Magick thing a shot.

I know I'm still far from understanding everything about his religion. But I finally don't feel as ignorant as I once did. I think that's why I got so upset when he called me naive that first night at O'Neill's—because deep down, I knew that I was. And that insecurity was too big to face then.

But now, with Liam's help, I can finally admit that all I needed was a little bit of grace and a lot of knowledge about a belief system I just wasn't used to.

Maybe I *am* starting to feel the Salem magic.

Just a little bit, though.

***

"I'm sorry, am I hearing you correctly right now?"

"It's the truth. I don't know what to tell you."

"So, these words are actually coming out of your mouth. I'm not hallucinating?"

"You're not hallucinating."

"And this isn't a nightmare?"

"Not that I'm aware of."

"Wow… and I thought we were just starting to become friends."

Liam chuckles and takes a sip of his coffee. We're sitting at our usual table at the Red Line Café.

"Listen, Blondie, you'd feel the same way if you were in my shoes."

I snort. "I could never deign to feel the way you feel in that fucked-up head of yours."

He rolls his eyes. "Look, the Tom Holland movies are just better. They are. There's no argument." He smirks smugly.

"I don't even understand how we're having this conversation right now. Tobey Maguire literally *created* the live-action Peter Parker out of thin air. He had no one to model his mannerisms on—the way he spoke, the way he moved. The others just carried on the legacy he started!" I say, getting a little too heated over an argument about *Spider-Man*, of all things.

"I'll give you this: Maguire was a great Peter Parker. And Garfield was a great Spider-Man. But Holland is the only one who's actually decent at *both*," Liam says simply with a shrug.

"I could honestly argue with you about this for hours." I sigh.

"Maybe we should just agree to disagree, then."

I glare at him, unwilling to compromise.

"For the sake of our friendship?" he adds, raising an eyebrow.

"...Fine," I finally concede. "But we're having a Tobey Maguire Spider-Man marathon one of these days so you can *revisit those* cinema classics and understand how *deadly* wrong you are."

He grins. "Deal. We can at least agree the crossover was pretty good, right?"

"...Yeah, okay. The crossover was fucking phenomenal." I relent with a grin. "Are you a big Marvel fan?" I ask, steering us into calmer waters.

"Sort of. Mostly the comic books. I used to read them after long days at the library in college," he says a little shyly.

I snicker and sip my coffee. He catches my look and frowns. "What?"

"Nothing."

"No, what is it?"

"It just makes sense, that's all." I shrug.

"What makes sense?"

"You. And comic books. I can already picture it—an Iron Man poster on your wall, a Spider-Man action figure on your dresser," I tease with a smirk.

"Hey. I never said anything about posters or action figures," he says, wagging a finger at me.

"Okay, all right," I say, holding up my hands in defense. "So that's what you did in college, huh?"

"Well, sometimes I'd read mystery novels instead of comic books," he admits, and it makes me smile.

"No, I mean like… you never went to parties or snuck into bars with a fake ID?"

He goes quiet for a moment before answering. "No. Not really. Wasn't my scene. Plus, I wasn't exactly the guy people invited out anyway. Some people find the whole

Wicca thing a little weird." He shrugs like it's no big deal, but it tugs at something inside me. Maybe it's guilt. After all, I judged him for his beliefs when we first met.

"On behalf of everyone who makes terrible snap judgments about people sometimes, I'm so sorry you had to deal with that," I say sincerely.

"It's okay. I honestly didn't mean you. At least you're trying to learn. For others, their biases are a little more deep-rooted, harder to break." He looks down at his coffee mug. I wonder if he's thinking about people in general or one person in particular.

"Did you go to a lot of parties in college?" he asks, clearly trying to redirect.

I chuckle, taking the hint that he doesn't want to talk about him anymore. "Yeah, a fair few. Lindsey and I were pretty wild, honestly." A few vivid memories flash in my mind.

"Hmm." He sips his coffee.

"What?" I glare at him.

"Nothing. It just makes sense, that's all," he says, smirking as he throws my own words back at me.

I laugh and shake my head. "We probably had too much fun sometimes. It was only ever a good time because I had Lindsey. When the parties ended and the bar lights turned on at 3 a.m., she was always the one I went home with. Always the one who showed up with coffee and aspirin the next morning. The rest of them... they were only friends when alcohol was involved."

"Did you keep in touch with anyone else after you graduated?" Liam asks.

"Nope. We tried a few times, but no one was really interested. Lindsey was smart to get out when she did. I got stuck for a while, making friends who turned out to be fake ones. Same cycle over and over."

"That's too bad," he says softly.

"That's New York." I shrug. "Everyone's always climbing a social ladder, looking for their next best connection. If you're not willing to help them climb higher, they don't hang around for very long."

He snorts. "No wonder you wanted a fresh start."

I nod in agreement.

Liam goes quiet for a second. Then he says, "Why did you leave New York? I know that's not the whole story. And I also know the reason you gave Damon on the boat last month was bullshit. So... tell me why."

There it is—the confrontation I've been dreading.

I take a deep breath and start talking before I can chicken out.

"The short answer is that I wanted more authenticity in my life. Which, I'm sure, is the 'bullshit' answer that you are referring to. The long answer is... I thought I was in love. I thought I'd found my future. Then, four years later, I found out he'd lied to me and cheated on me, and then, ultimately, kicked me out of our apartment. So... yeah. That's why." I'm completely mortified.

"Your boyfriend cheated on *you*?" Liam asks as if he's shocked to hear that could ever happen to me. Which is slightly flattering.

"Mm-hmm. With his assistant. Of all people." I smile tightly, blinking fast to hold back the tears that threaten to fall. "Honestly, I get it. She's younger, prettier, more vibrant, less opinionated. She probably laughs at all his jokes and doesn't call him out when he flirts with waitresses or forgets anniversaries. He's better off, really."

The tears slip free despite my best efforts.

"Anyway, that's my sob story. Should we see if they have any biscuits left? The biscuits here are amazing!" I start to stand, desperate to escape, but Liam reaches across the table and gently pulls me back down.

"Freya, stop."

"No, seriously, they're super good. And they go fast, so we should really—"

"Freya." His voice cuts through my rambling. "I'm so sorry. I had no idea." He reaches out and wipes the tears from my cheeks.

"Yeah, well. That was kind of the point. I didn't want anyone to know. Except Lindsey. She's the reason I had a place to land at all."

More tears slip out, and the words come pouring out.

"His name's Jackson. We met at the magazine I used to work at. He was a senior editor. We found this gorgeous apartment in SoHo—floor-to-ceiling windows, views of West Broadway... all the stuff you think matters when you feel like you've found your person. And now, some twenty-something tramp is sleeping in my silk sheets and having coffee in my breakfast nook every morning."

I cringe at my bitterness. "Sorry. I don't usually say stuff like that. I know it's not her fault."

"You can still call him a tramp if you want. I won't tell anyone," Liam says, dead serious.

I smile weakly at his loyalty. "Thanks. I'm fine, honestly. I just… I really thought he was the one. As cheesy and cliché as that sounds."

"And we all know how much you hate cheesy and cliché."

"Right." I chuckle weakly, a fresh wave of tears pricking my eyes. "After he told me, I just... I fell into a daze. I don't even know if I'm out of it yet. I think that's why I moved all the way out here. I wasn't thinking. I was just surviving."

"Well," he says, "are you happier for it?"

"For getting cheated on?"

"No. For moving to Massachusetts. Which city makes you happier?"

"Oh, Salem. One thousand percent. Even when you were a complete and utter dick to me when I first got here."

He laughs. "There's your answer then. Stop questioning whether or not it was the right decision to leave, and just embrace the fact that you did." It's so simple, coming from him. And somehow, it's exactly what I needed to hear.

"Thank you, Liam." I sniffle, wiping my face.

"And don't ever think you're worth less because of some jackass's mistakes. Any guy who takes you for granted doesn't deserve your tears."

He's staring at me so intently that it almost knocks the breath out of me.

I look away quickly, focusing on my coffee mug. "Well, good thing I only cried over you once."

He chuckles. "Yeah, good thing."

We sit in silence for a moment before I blurt out, "Sometimes, my head gets all twisted. I think about the man Jackson *used* to be… and that maybe one day, I can get that man back. The guy who bought me special gifts, gave me foot rubs when I had a long day, and actually listened when I told him how I felt. But then I have to snap back into reality. That man is gone, and there's no getting him back. I need to accept that."

Liam nods, his eyes never leaving mine.

"None of it matters anyway. I've shut myself off from love for the foreseeable future. Maybe forever. I don't even know if true love really exists. Y'know, like the kind they try to sell you in a romantic comedy. Or like what George and Mary have. Seems like a fickle dream to me."

"I can't help you much there," Liam says with a sigh. "I'm not so great at it myself."

There's a story there, I'm sure of it, but before I can ask, he asks me something instead.

"Do you know the origin of your name?"

I blink. "No... why?"

He shrugs. "Just wondering." He smiles and stands up. "I'll go get you that biscuit."

I watch him walk to the counter, a little confused by his question. But I forget about it after a minute as my mind begins mulling over everything that just spilled out of me. When he returns, he sets a strawberry scone down in front of me.

"They were out of biscuits."

"That's okay. Thank you." I smile, nibbling on the scone.

We sit in silence for a minute before I speak again.

"I know I made the right choice leaving. I didn't belong in New York. I just don't really know *where* I belong... I look at you, and I see someone who *knows* where they belong. You're lucky."

"Well," he says after a moment, "maybe you can belong here too."

I look up at him—he's staring down at his mug, too shy to make eye contact. I can't help the smile that spreads onto my face.

Now, *that's* a nice thought.

Chapter 9

October 2024

"Just hear me out," Lindsey says, following me like a puppy dog out of my room and into the kitchen. She's really getting on my last nerve right now—but in that way only your best friend can.

"The answer is still no. Nope. Nah. Negative. Nay. NO!" I yell, grabbing a bottle of red wine from the fridge and pouring myself a glass. I need a strong drink if I'm going to be subjected to this conversation.

"Seriously!? You don't feel one single, tiny, minuscule feeling for him?" she whines, flopping dramatically into one of the kitchen chairs.

"For the umpteenth time—no, I don't! I know that's hard for you to hear since you all love that man so goddamn much, but I can promise you I don't feel anything remotely resembling love, affection, romantic inklings, or sexual attraction for Liam fucking Doyle," I say, not wanting to argue anymore.

"Freya Whitney!" Lindsey gasps. "You know for a fact that he's a good guy, and I know for a fact you're in denial. I've seen the way you look at him, and I've seen the way he looks at you. It's just a matter of time before he gets down on one knee and you're picking out wedding china," she teases, a giant grin spreading across her face.

"I'd like you to please stop now," I say, but even I have to fight back a little smile. I head toward the bathroom to start my makeup and hair, hoping that's the end of it, but of course, she follows me. Lindsey's been ready for a half hour now, and I'm surprisingly behind schedule, so I need to move quickly if we're going to make it on time.

It's a tradition in the friend group to go to Salem's big Halloween bash at the old Town Hall every year. Live band, dancing, costume contests, bobbing for apples, fancy finger foods, and lots and lots of booze. By the time I was even made aware of the party, the tickets were, unsurprisingly, long gone. But thankfully for me, Lindsey had bought me a ticket in June, 'just in case I still happened to be here.' The only reason I'm tolerating this conversation right now is because I'm so grateful she thought to do that for me months ago. Otherwise, I'd have been left high and dry for plans tonight.

"You need to get back out there, Frey! You're so hot and smart. Anyone, especially Liam, would be psyched out of their mind if you went out with them."

"I'm not going on a date with Liam."

"But why—"

"I'm not going on a date with anyone!" I shout, opening my makeup bag and plugging in my straightener to heat it up. "Listen, Linds, I appreciate that you want to help me. But I'm done looking for love. I tried it, and it didn't work out for me. I've accepted my fate. I'll die happy and alone. Or sad and alone. With lots of cats," I joke, but there's a hint of sincerity in my words.

I'm not interested in putting myself in the position to get my heart broken again. It's not worth the possibility of finding another love. Not after what happened with Jackson.

"But even if I hadn't given up, I could never date someone like Liam Doyle," I conclude.

My phone starts buzzing, and I glance down to see that my dad is calling. I silence the call and continue applying my eye makeup. Not the best timing, Dad. I'm too busy yelling at my best friend.

"You don't just stop looking for love. Love finds you. Don't let something good walk away just because you're too hurt to fight for it. Seize the day! Chase your destiny!" she shouts in a prophetic tone.

"Thanks. I think that's enough clichés for today." I wave her off. "And y'know, you're one to talk."

"What's that supposed to mean?" She crosses her arms and leans against the bathroom door frame, feigning deep offense.

"Well, I don't exactly see you 'seizing the day' when it comes to you and Bailey." I make eye contact with her through the mirror and raise my eyebrow with a smirk.

"I do not know to what you are referring." Her response is stiff, but there's a telltale blush creeping up her neck.

"Oh, please, you do too."

"Do not!"

"Do too!"

"Do NOT!"

"Okay, this could go on for hours." I laugh.

Lindsey disappears from the threshold of the bathroom door, and I think I finally have a moment of peace.

But of course, she returns two seconds later, arms still crossed, with a pout on her face.

"Even if I did know what you were talking about. Which I don't—"

"Which you do."

"Even if I did—why would I listen to you? You're a terrible wingwoman."

I scoff. "What?! What are you talking about? I am an excellent wingwoman." I lower my mascara wand and turn around to face her, hand on my hip.

"You are not! Remember sophomore year when you thought that Chris Adams liked me? So I made a huge fool of myself asking him out, and it turns out he was gay and sleeping with the RA?"

Huh. I honestly forgot about that. A giggle escapes before I can help it. "Okay, fine. That was bad. But this time, I'm certain! Mark my words." I wag my finger at her before turning back around to continue with my makeup.

"Well, then you can mark my words about Liam," Lindsey adds with a snark, but her eyes are sparkling with amusement.

I sigh. "Let's just leave it at a difference of opinions."

"Fine," she agrees.

"Fine." At that, I slam the bathroom door in her face—but not before she sticks her tongue out at me through the gap. I let out a cackle before focusing on getting ready. Now I'm going to be the one who makes us late. I don't like the thought of that.

***

I think about what Lindsey said all the way to the party. My brain is circulating with questions. Why would she ever think Liam and I should date? Do the others think the same thing? I try to quiet my anxiety as we approach the entrance of the party, but it's almost impossible. And when I catch my first glimpse of Liam, it somehow gets even harder.

Outside the open double doors of the old Town Hall building, Damon, Bailey, Charlene, Jenna, and Liam all stand chatting in a circle. I'm immediately impressed with Charlene and Jenna's couple's costumes. Charlene is dressed in a green and white pinstriped Beetlejuice suit with a crazy wig and white face paint, while Jenna complements her by wearing Lydia Deetz's lacy red wedding dress. A perfect representation of the film.

"Wow! You guys look incredible," I say as I exchange hugs with them.

"So do you two! Very sexy." Charlene grins, holding my hand above my head and motioning for me to twirl. I spin around, letting my short pink skirt move with the breeze. I do feel pretty sexy in the tight corset, which shows off my cleavage just enough, still leaving a little to the imagination.

"We decided to run with the blonde-brunette duo idea again, just like we used to at school," Lindsey adds, adjusting her own skirt. She's wearing practically the same outfit as me, just black, with giant horns instead of a little tiara.

"I don't get it," Damon says, a confused look on his face.

"We're Maleficent and Sleeping Beauty, dumbass," Lindsey responds, clearly offended.

He shrugs. "Never saw it."

"Oh, please, yes you have! What are you two supposed to be, anyway? You don't even look like you're wearing costumes." She gestures at him and Liam. I have to admit, I'm not sure what they're supposed to be either—both of them seem to be wearing their regular clothes.

"I'm Damon. From *The Vampire Diaries*," Damon says, gripping the edges of his black leather jacket and giving us a little spin. Underneath, he's wearing a gray T-shirt and black skinny jeans.

"That's pathetic! At least Bailey actually dressed up," Lindsey says, gesturing to him. Bailey's face lights up more than I ever thought possible.

"Thanks, Linds," he says with a smile. They make eye contact, and she gives him an uncharacteristically shy grin in return.

"You're welcome. You look very handsome, Mr. Holmes," she says, playfully adjusting his detective cap. He really does look dapper in his three-piece suit, and the pipe in his mouth is the perfect added touch of authenticity.

"Have you ever even seen that show?" Charlene questions Damon, still clearly unimpressed with his effort.

"I've seen an episode. I think," Damon says defensively. "And everyone always says I look like him, which I think is pretty fitting since we have the same name." He flashes a prideful smirk.

Liam snorts loudly. "Yeah, sure. You'd look exactly like him if you squint really hard and turn off all the lights. Who has ever told you that?"

"Uh–lots of people that you don't happen to know," Damon huffs, turning to go inside the building.

We all burst out laughing before following him through the doors. Charlene and Jenna run to catch up with the drama queen, while Bailey and Lindsey fall into natural conversation. I can't help but think how cute a couple they would make. Why can't Lindsey focus on her own love life and leave mine alone?

My thoughts are interrupted when I feel a hand land on my shoulder. "Hey," Liam says with a small smile. Speak of the devil.

"Hey!" I say back, probably a little too excited. We fall into step behind the rest of the group, walking down a very well-decorated hallway. I can hear the music of the band and the chatter of a large crowd getting louder with every step.

"I'm exci—" I start to say, but stop quickly when Liam starts speaking at the same time.

"You look great," he says quickly. "Sorry. Uh, what were you saying?" His cheeks turn slightly pink, and I giggle at his sheepish apology.

"It's okay. And thank you! I was just saying I'm excited about this party. Lindsey's been hyping it up all day," I say as we finally enter the large banquet hall.

It's packed with people in all kinds of amazing

costumes. Long tables line each side of the giant room, stacked high with delicious-looking hors d'oeuvres and snacks. I count at least five bars, and that's just the ones I can see. Across the room, a funky band dressed like mummies is jamming out to Frank Sinatra's "Witchcraft," and in the center, hundreds of people are already dancing. Fake cobwebs drape every wall, with witches, spiders, scarecrows, and skeletons filling every spare corner. Hundreds of flickering candles add a spooky ambiance to the room, and a huge disco ball over the dance floor throws sparkling light everywhere.

"This is insane!" I shout over the music.

"It is pretty cool," Liam agrees. We stand side by side, taking it all in. Somehow, we've already lost our friends in the crowd.

"Would you like a drink?" he asks, glancing down at me and nodding toward the nearest bar. The line's already crazy long.

"Yeah. I'll come with you," I say, and we make our way to stand at the back of the line.

"How's work been?" Liam asks.

"Really good, actually," I say, feeling a flutter of excitement. "I just started a piece I think you'd be interested in. It's for a Halloween-themed column. I'm doing a human-interest story on Salem's most haunted houses. Not the tourist traps, though. I'm focusing on local families who've lived in supposedly haunted homes for generations. Real stories about what it's like growing up in a place the whole town whispers about."

Liam's face lights up. "That sounds awesome. If you need help with research, I'm sure I could dig up some old stories in our archives."

"I was actually hoping to interview you," I say, energized by his enthusiasm. "Y'know, for a local expert's take on the subject."

"I would love that." He grins and lets out a little chuckle. "Do my eyes deceive me, or is Freya Whitney finally warming up to Salem's spooky side?"

I throw up my hands in defense. "Listen, I'm just writing what the people want. It's my journalistic duty to set aside personal beliefs and follow the story… even if that story happens to be about ghosts."

"Whatever you say," he says with a playful eye roll.

"I have to admit, though—some of the things I've heard are keeping me up at night. I've resorted to sleeping with my closet light on," I add with a mock shudder. "If you find me hiding under my bed tomorrow, you'll know why."

"Don't worry, I'll come protect you. Armed with some sage, obviously," he teases.

I laugh, feeling a warm flutter in my chest. Somehow, with Liam, even ghost talk feels easy.

"So, do Wiccans not have a holiday they celebrate on Halloween?" I ask, curious. "I would think tonight would be your biggest night of the year."

"We do. It's called Samhain. Celebrations usually start tonight and carry into tomorrow," he says simply.

"Does it entail you flying over the streets of Salem on your broomstick later this evening? Because if so, I'd love a ride home after the party," I say with a wink. Thankfully, he laughs.

"Unfortunately, no broomsticks will be used tonight. Samhain marks the end of the harvest season and the beginning of the winter months. Usually, I have a big dinner with my family, and we build an altar to honor our ancestors. It's supposed to be the one day of the year when it's easiest for the dead to cross over the veil and visit the mortal world, so it's important to celebrate those who have passed."

"It's like Day of the Dead?" I ask.

"Exactly. That's one of the holidays that originated

from the same roots. Halloween, too."

We move up further in the slow line.

"Why are you out tonight if your family is celebrating?" I ask, confused as to why he's missing tonight's holiday when he hasn't missed any of the other ones since I've met him.

"I'll celebrate with them tomorrow. Usually, I don't come to this party with everyone. But, I guess this year I wanted to join in." He shrugs. I can't tell if he's telling the whole truth, but I decide not to press him.

"Hey, you never said… What's your costume?" I look him over, trying to piece it together. He's wearing a blue striped button-down, dark jeans, and a gray sweatshirt.

"Oh, here." He pulls a pair of glasses out of his jacket pocket, which definitely aren't his—or at least if they are, I've never seen him wear them before—and slides them on before stepping back with his arms out.

"Uuuhh… are you… an overworked college student about to cram for finals?" I joke.

"Nope."

"Okay, I give up. Who are you?"

"I'll give you one more hint." He starts to unbutton the top few buttons of his shirt. I'm not sure why, but my stomach jumps a little at the small sliver of skin he reveals underneath. At first, I'm slightly confused as to what he's doing. But then, it all finally clicks as he undoes one more button, and I see a little bit of red fabric peek out from under his shirt. Somehow, my stomach jumps even more than it did before.

"Well, Peter Parker, it's a pleasure," I say with a laugh, extending my hand.

He shakes it firmly. "The pleasure's all mine, Sleeping Beauty. Or Aurora… which does she prefer?" he teases, whispering the last bit like it's a grave offense to get it wrong.

"Aurora is fine for her close friends," I say, winking. He grins wider and drops my hand, turning back toward the bar as we near the front.

"That's a very clever costume, by the way," I add, giving him another once-over. I can tell he modeled it after Tobey Maguire's version, though I don't say it out loud.

"Thanks. Probably won't win any contests, but I thought it was a little better than Damon's, at least," he says modestly.

"I think any costume is better than Damon's." I giggle.

***

After grabbing our drinks and a few snacks to munch on, Liam and I meet the rest of the group at a high-top table that they somehow managed to snag on the edge of the dance floor. It's a perfect people-watching spot. We sip our drinks and nibble things off our small plates while the band continues to play. Eventually, Charlene gets all the girls out onto the dance floor. It doesn't take much convincing since at this point, I've had more than a couple of drinks. It's easy to feel the music pulse through my body as I let myself get lost in the melody and move however I'm feeling.

Damon joins us soon enough, stealing any spotlight we may have garnered, deservedly so, with his surprisingly limber dance moves. When Lindsey drags Bailey out to dance with her, I glance back at our table and spot Liam standing there alone, sipping his drink and looking anywhere but at me.

A slight twinge grips my heart, similar to the one I felt the day I saw him sitting alone on the boat over the summer. I didn't do anything about it then, but this time, I know I should.

I leave the group on the dance floor and head back to the table. Liam turns and gives me a small smile as I grab my drink and take a little sip, pretending that was the reason I came over.

"Are you using your spidey senses to guard our table?" I ask.

"I have to be vigilant if I'm going to stand here alone. It's an ideal spot. Don't want anyone sneaking in to steal it while you're all out on the floor," he says, a hint of something akin to sadness in his voice.

"Well, I think you might be safe to come dance for just one song."

"No, it's okay. I don't mind holding down the fort," he says.

"C'mon! It looks like most people are dancing anyway, so I doubt anyone will steal it, especially with Bailey's and Damon's coats here." I gesture to their discarded garments. Really, though, I just don't want him to be alone. Sometimes, it feels like he's always the one expected to give up having a good time for the sake of the group. And I don't think that's very fair, no matter how many times he says it's okay.

"Really, Freya. It's all good. Go have fun." He points to the dance floor with a kind smile.

"Well, I wanna have fun with you! What, you don't

dance?" I ask.

"As a matter of fact, no. I don't," he says.

"Oh, come on. Everyone likes to dance!"

"Not me."

"Have you ever done it before?"

"This might surprise you, but yes, I have. A few times, actually. I'm not incapable of participating in fun activities, y'know," he says, with a little bite to his words.

"I know that. I just think you have such a large stick up your ass that when you do participate in said activities, you don't know how to actually enjoy them. That's why all your friends are out on the dance floor and you're standing here guarding their coats." I cross my arms and tap my foot. I'm not going to let this one go. He deserves to have a little fun, too.

"Freya, please. Just—"

"No. Y'know what? I'm going to do something for you tonight. You've taught me so much over the past couple of months, and now it's my turn to teach you something."

"And what would that be? How to do the Cha Cha Slide?"

"No. How to let loose. Relax. Live a little! Are you familiar with these terms? It's what normal people say when they want to stop being so serious and have fun."

"Yes, I think I've heard of them before," he says, trying to stay stoic, but I can see a tiny smile creeping at the corners of his mouth.

"Great! So come and dance with me! It's Halloween, and I want you to at least enjoy it a little bit… Do it for me?" I break out the puppy dog eyes.

He stands there in silence for a few seconds, keeping strong eye contact with me, giving me a look that's pleading with me to stop. But then, I see his miraculously green eyes soften slightly before he closes them and drops his head with a sigh. He places his glass down on the table.

"Fine," Liam says, picking his head back up to look at me again. "But if they start playing 'Monster Mash,' I'm done."

I laugh. "Okay. Deal." I scoop his hand up in mine and lead him out to where our friends are on the dance floor.

The band slows their pace from the swinging song they were just playing to a smoother and soulful piece, one that I recognize. The lead singer starts crooning the first line of "I Put a Spell on You" just as Liam and I land in the middle of the crowd. I notice Bailey and Lindsey have wrapped their arms around each other as they sway to the music, their chemistry obvious to anyone looking.

When I glance back at Liam, he has his left hand extended out to me and his right arm tucked behind his back, wordlessly inviting me into a dance. I take his hand, and he pulls me into frame, his other hand settling firmly on my mid-back. I place my left hand on his broad shoulder, and we start to sway to the jazzy waltz.

Liam effortlessly leads me, his hand bringing me closer and closer to him with each step. God, he's so tall, I have to crane my neck up to actually look him in the eye, even in my heels. I let out a surprised giggle when he pushes me out into a spin and then pulls me back into his body.

"Okay, I'll take it back. You do know how to move your feet a bit," I say, slightly stunned.

He chuckles and looks down at the floor before meeting my eyes again.

"Well, as shocking as it may seem, I do know how to, uh—how did you phrase it—'let loose' and 'live a little,'" he says, a teasing smirk on his face.

"All right, maybe I was a little tough on you. But sometimes, it just seems like you isolate yourself because, for some reason, you feel like you have to, even though you don't really want to?" I say hesitantly, ending the sentence like a question.

He rolls his eyes. "No. I do not do that… Okay, fine. Sometimes I may do that," he admits.

"Why?" I ask.

"Well, I just… I don't know. I guess I feel bad if I think everyone isn't having as much fun as they can be, so I do everything in my power to make sure they do—even if that means I don't." He shrugs.

"That's surprisingly really selfless of you."

"Surprisingly?" he retorts, eyebrows shooting up toward his hairline. I can't stop myself laughing.

"All right, Miss Twinkle Toes… just shut up and enjoy the music," he says, shaking his head but smiling down at me.

The sultry song winds deeper into its melody. Liam's hand slides a little lower down my back, his fingers curling into my spine and sending a shiver up and down my body. My right hand grips his left as he starts to turn us in a slow circle, keeping our steady sway going. Our bodies pull even closer, until I find myself nuzzling into the nook between his neck and his shoulder.

A weird, warm fuzz starts swirling low in my stomach, and my palms begin to sweat. I'm nervous. Why am I nervous? It's just Liam, I remind myself. Stupid, obnoxious, arrogant, witty, intelligent, secretly caring, and thoughtful Liam. Liam, whom I used to hate with every particle of my body. Liam, who is now so close, I can feel his heartbeat against my chest, his breath warm against my cheek.

I pull my head away slightly and look back up at him. Our gazes meet again, and his eyes pierce through mine like they're trying to tell me something I can't quite figure out.

I get lost in every feature on his face—the color of his irises, the curve of his long nose, the sharp structure of his cheekbones, the wide cut of his jaw. Every bit is entirely too mesmerizing.

I realize we've stopped swaying altogether. We just stand there, holding each other, surrounded by people who are too lost in the music to notice.

I feel the electricity swirling between us again, something I've felt a few times before. When he touches me. When he looks at me the way he is right now. But I still can't figure out why it's there.

Then, clapping. Applauding. The band finishes the song, and everyone around us stops dancing to cheer.

Before I can wrap my head around what just

happened, the moment is broken.

I drop my gaze to my feet and step out of Liam's arms, turning toward the stage and clapping along with the crowd. I can still feel his eyes on me, but after a second, he turns as well.

I force a grin onto my face to hide the confusing cloud of feelings brewing inside me. "Well, that was really fun! Thank you for the dance," I say, trying to sound breezy.

He stares at me for a second before responding. "I'm just glad it wasn't 'Monster Mash,'" he says with a shy smile.

I laugh. "All right, c'mon, grumpy. Let's get another drink."

I turn around quickly, needing the alcohol to drown the feelings stirring in my chest.

When we get back to the table, Charlene, Jenna, and Damon are there, chatting with a girl with brown hair I don't recognize. Charlene grins at us as we join them, new drinks in hand.

"Hey! Where are Lindsey and Bailey?" I ask, realizing they aren't nearby.

"Oh, they're still grinding up on each other on the dance floor," Damon says, sounding thoroughly disgusted.

"Really?" I ask, slightly shocked and very excited by this turn of events. I turn back toward the crowd, scanning for them, and sure enough, there they are, doing exactly what Damon described, as the band transitions into a more upbeat song. Lindsey has her arms draped around Bailey's shoulders, while Bailey's hands rest securely on Lindsey's hips. They're laughing and moving together like they're the only two people in the room.

I nudge Liam with my elbow. "Look at them! They're adorable."

He follows my gaze and lets out a short chuckle. "'Adorable' is one word for it. Damon's clearly scarred for life, though."

"Hey, don't knock it! True love in the making over there," I say with a teasing smile.

Damon groans dramatically. "If I have to witness one more lingering eye stare or shy smile, I'm gonna lose it."

I giggle, turning back to the table, and I make eye contact with the girl I haven't had the pleasure of meeting yet. I give her a bright smile, and she returns it with a closed-lip smirk. Her eyes flick to my left to give Liam a once-over before turning back to Charlene. Got it, message received.

I sneak a glance at Liam, but it seems like he didn't even notice her flirty look. I smile to myself at the thought of him being so enchanted by the energy of the room that he's completely oblivious to the cute girl making eyes at him from across the table. It probably shouldn't make me happy, but it does.

"Liam! I want you to meet my friend, Samantha. We used to work together at my old company. Samantha, this is Liam. We've known each other since we were kids," Charlene says, gesturing between Liam and Samantha to introduce them.

"It's nice to meet you," Liam says, extending his hand. She takes it and gives it a small shake.

"You too! I've heard a lot about you. I have to say, you're a lot cuter than how Charlene described you," she says with a little giggle.

Liam looks down at the table for a second, his cheeks burning red. "Oh, uh—thank you," he says with a chuckle. "Uh—have you met our friend Freya?" he adds, pointing in my direction.

I turn and smile at Samantha again. "Hi! Nice to meet you," I say.

"Hi," she says quickly, giving me a brief smile before

turning back to Liam.

"So, would you like to go grab a drink, Liam? Or maybe some dessert if you already have a drink?" Samantha asks, completely ignoring me.

"Oh, well, I uh—"

"He would love to!" Charlene answers for him.

The two make eye contact for a second. Liam looks like he's trying to argue silently with her, but Charlene's expression is all but begging him to go.

"...Yeah, sure. That would be great," Liam finally says, turning back to Samantha.

"Great!" she chirps, heading toward one of the dessert tables. Liam hesitates for a moment, glancing quickly in my direction. Again, I'm not sure what his eyes are trying to tell me, but whatever the message is, I smile and shoo him along. He looks down briefly, then meets my eyes again with a small smile before following Samantha.

"See that! He likes her!" Charlene says, watching them interact. I follow her gaze and catch them chatting. But when Samantha throws her head back with a big, dramatic laugh, I have to tear my eyes away.

"Eh, I don't know. She seems a little too... peppy for him," Damon says, glancing over his shoulder.

"Well, it's not like he's going to marry her. He just needs a bit of a fling, that's all. Or a healthy one-night stand," Jenna says with a shrug, sipping her drink.

"Exactly! He needs to get back out there. It's been too long. You know that, Damon," Charlene adds, giving him a serious look. Damon just nods and turns back to the table.

For some reason, this conversation fills me with the utmost dread and anxiety. As much as I'd love to stand here and listen to my friends talk about a possible hookup for Liam, I need to leave before all the drinks and food I've consumed this evening come back up all over the floor.

"Y'know what, guys, I think I'm going to take off for the night. I'm starting to get really tired. I think I may have had one too many Love Potions," I say, holding up my empty glass.

"Aww, are you sure? We'll miss you," Charlene says as she circles the table to give me a hug.

I chuckle and assure her I'm sure. We pull apart, and I start getting my coat on.

"Honestly, we're probably not too far behind you," Jenna says, giving me a quick hug.

"Are you kidding? I still have at least another hour of dancing left in me," Charlene says.

"Take me with you," Damon jokes, looking deep into my eyes, pleading for an escape.

I laugh and pull him in for a hug goodbye. I glance over to where Lindsey and Bailey are still dancing and let out another laugh. I'm already looking forward to the moment I get to say "I told you so."

"Well, I won't interrupt the lovebirds over there. When they finally take a break, tell Lindsey I'll see her at home," I say with a smirk.

Finally, I glance back at Liam. He's still listening intently as Samantha talks, the space between them almost nonexistent as she leans in to speak into his ear over the loud music.

"You can tell Liam I left, too. Don't want to stop their budding romance either," I say, raising my eyebrows.

Charlene looks over her shoulder at the two of them nestled close.

"I knew it! See, they're falling in love as we speak," she says excitedly, downing the rest of her drink. "I'm going to grab another. Need anything, hon?" she asks Jenna sweetly.

"I'm all set, babe," Jenna says, holding up her still half-full glass.

Charlene gives her a quick kiss before heading toward the bar.

"Well, I'll see you guys later. Happy Halloween!" I wave.

They send me a chorus of goodbyes and Happy Halloweens as I turn to weave through the crowd toward the exit. At the doors, I turn back for one last look. Liam and Samantha are still deep in conversation, closer than before. I don't know what I thought I would see, but somehow, the sight still stings.

I turn and walk down the long hallway and out the front doors of the old Town Hall. The cold air immediately bites at my skin, a harsh breeze whipping through my hair. I try to feel happy for Liam. It seems like he likes Samantha, and she most definitely likes him.

In all the time I've known him, I've never once seen him even glance at a girl outside our friend group. Let alone talk to one who's clearly flirting. As his friend, I should be excited that he's putting himself out there.

But there's a small part of me, deep down, that feels disappointed.

For a second, on the dance floor, I thought maybe Lindsey was right. Maybe there was something between us.

Maybe he did have feelings for me, and I was just too blind to see them.

Obviously, I was wrong.

Probably for the better anyway. There's no way Liam and I could ever make something work. Ever.

At least, that's what I tell myself as I walk through the dark backstreets of Salem, shivering in my miniskirt. In hindsight, maybe not the most practical costume choice.

In a small moment of desperation, my thoughts drift back to what Liam said about Magick and positive thinking. I'm still skeptical, and honestly not even sure if it's supposed to be used in this way. After all, I probably can't will something into existence if it isn't meant to be... but, what do I have to lose?

So I try it. I picture Liam and me together—laughing, holding each other, looking into his eyes just like I had done while we danced. I focus my mind and really try to believe it's real. A warm tingle pulses through me, and for a second, I can almost feel his arms around my waist again. And I feel... happy.

A car alarm blares nearby, yanking me out of the moment. The image dissolves instantly, the warmth gone just as fast, leaving me cold and alone on the sidewalk.

I don't know what I thought would happen. That he'd magically appear beside me with a bouquet of flowers? That time would rewind, and we'd be back on the dance floor, swaying like Samantha had never shown up?

Stupid. I feel stupid. But more than that, I feel embarrassed—because some part of me *wanted* it to work. And that means some part of me might actually… like Liam.

The second that thought forms, I shove it deep down, burying it so fast I almost convince myself it was never there.

When I get back to the apartment, I quickly change into a cozy pair of pajamas and take off my makeup. I crawl into bed and queue up an episode of *Friends* to watch on my laptop before falling asleep.

Monica and Chandler's love story always comforts me when I'm feeling down about my own nonexistent love life, which, frankly, happens more often than I'd like to admit. I've watched this show too many times.

Snuggling under the duvet, I hit the space bar on my laptop to start the episode, just as my phone buzzes on the mattress beside me.

As I pick it up, I'm expecting to see Lindsey's name with a text asking if I made it home okay. But when my eyes adjust to the brightness, I'm surprised to see the name on the screen:

Liam
Charlene said you left? Are you okay?

Freya
Yeah, I'm fine. Just got really tired all of a sudden. I'm home now, in bed, watching Friends.

Liam
Ah, why am I not surprised?

Freya
It's a good show!

Liam
Whatever you say.

I giggle at his response. The little incoming text bubble appears and disappears a few times before his next message pops up.

Liam
Are you sure you're okay?

I hesitate for a second before typing back.

Freya

Yeah, of course! Now stop texting me and pay attention to Samantha. If you play your cards right, you might even get laid tonight ;)

Liam
Right. My mission in life. Well, I'll see you soon, I guess.

Freya
Yeah, totally! Have a good rest of your night.

Liam
I will, thank you. You too.

I put my phone down and try to focus back on the episode.

I don't even bother asking if he wants to get coffee tomorrow. Even though it's Sunday, I assume he'll be too busy, wrapped up with the beautiful, naked Samantha twisted in his bedsheets after a night of blissful lovemaking.

I push the image out of my mind just as my phone buzzes again.

Liam
Happy Halloween, Freya.

Freya
Happy Halloween, Liam.

Chapter 10

The next morning, I stumble out of my room in a fog. My head is pounding. Maybe I *did* drink too much. I guess my excuse to leave last night was more legitimate than I thought.

I shuffle into the bathroom, grab the bottle of aspirin from the medicine cabinet, and dry swallow two pills before heading toward the kitchen in search of caffeine.

As I pass through the kitchen doorway, I make a beeline for the coffee machine, already full with a fresh pot. Thank God for Lindsey.

"Morning, Freya."

"Morning, Bai—" I start to automatically respond as I reach for a mug in the cabinet. Then I freeze mid-motion, fingers still on the handle, as my brain catches up with my words.

I slam the cabinet shut and whip my head to the side. Yep. There he is. Bailey. Sitting at our kitchen table with a cup of coffee and the Sunday paper.

"I—uh. Don't take this the wrong way, but… did you sleep here?" I ask, squinting at him like he might dissolve into mist.

"Yep," he replies casually, flipping a page like he's been doing this every weekend.

"You slept over," I repeat slowly. "Okay. Sure. Makes sense. Excuse me for a moment."

I place the mug gently on the counter and start walking toward the door, just as it swings open. Lindsey steps through, wearing her hair in a messy bun and, notably, Bailey's dress shirt from last night.

"Oh, heyyy roomie," she says breezily, squeezing past me to grab the mug I left behind. She fills it with coffee and heads over to the table, where she gives Bailey a quick peck before sitting down.

I stay rooted in place, blinking like I've forgotten how to function as a person. My brain hasn't finished buffering this whole situation. I need coffee.

"So we're just gonna carry on like this is a totally normal Sunday morning?" I ask, grabbing another mug and filling it up.

"Yep," Bailey says again, still not bothering to look up.

"Pretty much," Lindsey echoes, equally unfazed.

"Cool. Well, just for the record, Linds—I was right," I say, hopping up onto the counter and taking a victorious sip.

"Fine." She sighs, giving me an unimpressed look. "For *this one time*, I can admit that you may have been right about something to do with my love life. Happy now?"

"Very." I grin. "So, how were Liam and Samantha at the end of the night? Did he whisk her away for a magical evening back at his place?" I joke, though the words taste a little sour on the way out.

"Who?" Lindsey frowns.

"What do you mean *who*? Liam Doyle."

"Yeah, I know who Liam is, but who's Samantha?"

"The girl Charlene introduced to him. Last night at the party. Brown hair? Tall? Really pretty? *Samantha*?" I say, like I'm hosting a game of Guess Who.

"We didn't meet anyone named Samantha," Bailey chimes in, finally looking up from his paper.

"Huh. Weird. They seemed super into each other." Now I'm the confused one.

"Oh! You mean Samantha from Charlene's old office?" Lindsey asks.

"Yes! That one. When I left, they were snuggled up pretty close at the dessert table."

"That's the girl Charlene's been trying to set him up with for the past month. He keeps refusing to take her number. I *knew* she'd pull something sneaky." Lindsey swats at Bailey's arm. Apparently, I'm not the only target of Charlene's matchmaking efforts.

"But you didn't *see* her last night?" I ask.

"Nope. By the time we got back to the table, you were gone, Damon was drunk, and Liam was alone. He looked kind of... sad, actually. Did you say something to him?" Lindsey raises an eyebrow at me.

"What? No!" I defend myself.

"Well, all I know is Liam was definitely sulking after you left," she says pointedly, like she's turning the tables on me. Which is not fair. *I'm* supposed to be the one saying "I told you so" today. But I'm too distracted to argue.

My mind keeps circling back to the fact that I walked out of that party without saying goodbye to Liam, because I assumed he ditched me for someone else. Which, in hindsight, wasn't exactly rational. It's not like he's my boyfriend. We're not dating. Not even close.

And yet… I was upset. Why?

Because friends should be happy for each other when they meet someone. That's why I left. Because I was happy for him. Totally. Absolutely.

"Weren't you two meeting for coffee today?" Bailey asks, flipping back to his paper like it's no big deal.

Wait—*coffee.*

Oh my God.

My hangover evaporates on the spot. I glance at the clock, and panic sets in. It's already ten past nine. Which means I'm already ten minutes late.

"Shit!" I nearly spill my coffee as I slam it onto the counter and bolt from the room. I throw on clothes in record time—probably not my best look, but I don't have the luxury to care. Wool plaid jacket, boots—go, go, go.

I shout a rushed goodbye to Bailey and Lindsey on my way out, but don't wait for a response as I hurl myself down the stairs two at a time.

I sprint through Salem's winding back streets, dodging tourists still lingering from the holiday, darting past whimsical shop windows and sidewalk cafés.

By the time I reach Red Line Café, it's already 9:30. I whip open the front door in a frenzy, just in time to crash chest-first into someone walking out.

"I'm so sorry, I—"

"You and I are really making a habit of literally running into each other."

I look up and meet a pair of familiar green eyes. Of *course* it's Liam. And of *course* he was about to leave. Because of *course* I'm a dumbass who made a bunch of assumptions I had no right to make.

"You're leaving," I say, breathless.

He sighs. "Yeah."

"Because you thought I wasn't coming."

"...Yeah."

"Because I'm an idiot who left you last night without even saying goodbye."

"...Yep. Pretty much."

I groan. "I'm *so* sorry, Liam. I didn't mean to make you think I blew you off. I just—last night, from where I stood, it looked like you and Samantha were getting along, and I figured you'd rather spend the night with a cute girl than have me hovering around getting in the way. So I left." It all comes tumbling out before I can stop myself.

Liam lets out a soft chuckle and places his hand on my shoulder, giving it a gentle squeeze. It's grounding, and I think he knows it.

"Freya, it's okay. Honestly. Just breathe. I'm not mad at you."

I let out a long, shaky breath. "You're not?"

"No. I mean, I *was* a little bummed this morning when I thought you weren't coming. But now that I know what was going through your head, I get it. You still want to grab that coffee?"

"Well, I *did* run all the way here from my apartment, so if I don't at least get *one* cup of coffee with you, it would have all been for nothing, and I don't think I can accept that."

"All right." He laughs as he lightly presses a hand to the small of my back and guides me through the café door.

"This one's on me," I say, tossing him a smile over my shoulder.

"I won't say no to a free coffee," He says before scouting out a spot by the window while I head to the counter to order.

A few minutes later, I join Liam with two mugs in hand.

"Thank you," he says as he takes one.

"You're welcome." I sit across from him, and we both sip in comfortable silence for a moment. Then he sets his mug down and looks at me.

"For the record… I never considered going home with Samantha. Charlene's always trying to set me up, but I don't think I've ever actually gone out with anyone she's picked."

"Why not?" I ask. "She seemed like a nice enough girl. Cute. One-night stand material at least." I shrug.

"This may come as a shock to you," he says, raising an eyebrow, "but I don't base my entire life around finding people to sleep with."

"Well, yeah. I know that. But we're still human. We all have needs. Sometimes those needs need to be met, even if it's just for a night with someone you'll never see again."

He sips his coffee and gives me a look. "Do *you* have needs?"

I almost choke. "Me?"

"No," he deadpans, gesturing to the table next to us. "The old lady sitting to your right. Yes, *you*. The entire time I've known you, I haven't seen you try to get your *needs met* by anyone."

It doesn't escape my attention that he's dodging my original question, but I let it go. Clearly, this isn't the moment for straight answers.

"Well, I don't need a man to get my needs met anymore," I say, lifting my chin with a little extra sass. "I can do it perfectly fine by myself."

It isn't until I see Liam's eyebrows shoot up and a grin stretch across his face like he's just won the lottery that I realize what I've implied.

"Okay, hold on—that's not what I meant," I say quickly.

"No, no, I totally get it." He puts his hands up as if waving off any correction. "You are a self-sufficient, independent woman, and you can take care of your needs *all by yourself*. It's very admirable."

"Please, please, please stop," I groan, burying my face in my hands.

But he's not done.

"No, really, Freya. I might have to take a page out of your book. We're all human. We all have needs, right?" He leans back in his chair, enjoying this far too much. "In fact, I might think about you meeting *your* needs the next time I meet *mine*. Could give me that much-needed inspiration I've been looking for."

I let out another loud groan, my face on fire. "You're the worst."

"Aw, don't be like that, Frey. You're helping me. Seriously."

"I'd like to change the subject now, please."

It doesn't escape me that the positive thinking—or manifestation, or Magick, or whatever brand of cosmic meddling I attempted on my walk home last night—might have actually worked. Because here we are, just like before: together, laughing and talking, and no Samantha in sight.

Of course, I'm not about to mention this to Liam. He doesn't need to know I may have accidentally (or not-so-accidentally) wished his date away so he'd end up here with me instead. I've chalked it up to a moment of delusion, sparked by a mix of alcohol, Lindsey's relentless teasing, and the inconvenient fact that I haven't had a date in months. And I leave it at that.

Julia E. Christian

***

After Halloween, things go back to normal. Or at least, the version of normal that we've grown used to. The vibrant reds and oranges of October foliage begin to dull into shades of brown, scattering across the sidewalks and streets. Salem becomes blanketed in dry, crunchy leaves. I love the satisfying pop they make under my boots as I walk through town, like tiny fireworks beneath my feet.

With October behind us, the city breathes a little easier. The crowds have thinned out, the traffic has eased, and Salem has returned to its everyday chaos. I survived my first Halloween season here, and honestly? It wasn't nearly as bad as people warned. Sure, the lines were longer and the roads were clogged, but it was kind of charming to see the city packed with people who genuinely adore it.

Salem's tourists are different from the ones I used to dodge in New York—those wide-eyed crowds chasing celebrity sightings or ticking off movie locations. Here, people come for the history, the cozy autumn atmosphere, and the spirited locals who serve up the best stories. And yes, the witch memorabilia too. Can't forget that.

November means Scorpio season, which also means we celebrated our favorite tour guide's thirtieth birthday.

Liam insisted he didn't want anything big, so naturally, we broke into his apartment and threw him a surprise party. He claimed to be annoyed, but I could tell he was happy. I like seeing him happy.

The biggest change of the last few weeks, though, is that Lindsey and Bailey are now officially dating. I promised Lindsey I would stop gloating over the fact that I was right about Bailey being in love with her, but I still like to slip in a little teasing remark here and there. I can't deny they make an insanely cute couple.

The month has gone by so fast, and somehow it's already Thanksgiving. For the first time in probably my whole life, I'm actually looking forward to the holiday, because I'm not stuck celebrating it with my family. When Lindsey suggested we do a Friendsgiving this year, I was all for it. Mostly because it gave me a great excuse to tell my parents when they asked why I wasn't coming home for the weekend.

Sorry, Mom and Dad, but friends take precedence this year. And my mental health.

At least, that's what I keep telling myself during our hour-and-a-half-long car ride up Route 93 to New Hampshire.

"I really hope this Airbnb has decent sheets. I can't stand when they have those cheap cotton ones from Target," Damon says from the third row of the minivan. In order to fit all of us in one car, Lindsey borrowed her mom's Toyota for the weekend.

"*Ow!* Don't elbow me!" Damon shouts.

"Well, don't say weird shit like that," Liam replies calmly. He has the misfortune of sitting in the way back next to Damon for the drive up. We all played noses for it, and they lost fair and square.

"It's a nice place, I promise," Lindsey says from the front passenger seat. "One of the teachers at school recommended it to me. She and her family stayed there last year for the holidays and said they loved it. It's secluded in the woods near the lake but only a quick ten-minute drive from Portsmouth."

Bailey, the good boyfriend that he is, offered to drive (very slowly, might I add) so she could relax after a few long days at work prepping for the school's winter concert.

Jenna, Charlene, and I have been squished together in the middle row of the car for about an hour now. It might *seem* like a big car, but these seats are deceivingly close together. Thankfully, I got the window seat. We stuck

Charlene in the middle, and she's been paying for it—every few minutes, Damon pulls at her hair or flicks the back of her head to keep himself busy.

"Damon, I swear to God. If you lay another finger on me, you won't have it anymore," Charlene fumes after he tugs her long, dark locks again.

"I'm sorry! I'm bored!" he shouts.

"We're almost there, Damon. Just hang in there for like twenty more minutes," Lindsey says from the front, trying to comfort him.

"Tell that to Charlene," he mutters under his breath.

"Damon, you better—" Charlene starts, but she's interrupted by Bailey.

"Hey! If you two don't stop it, I will turn this damn car right around. Then no one gets any turkey. Don't test me, I'll do it," he says, glaring at them through the rearview mirror.

"Yes, Daddy," Damon says, teasing him. I chuckle a little and shake my head.

About twenty minutes later, we're finally pulling into the driveway of a small log cabin in the woods outside Portsmouth, New Hampshire. I open the door on my side and step out, taking a deep breath to smell the earthy aromas and dead leaves that fill the forest air. It's one of the best smells in the world, if you ask me. I walk toward the house and look up at the beautiful two-story log cabin. It has a huge wrap-around porch and looks like it has a great view of the lake down below from the back.

"Hey, Blondie! You wanna help us with the bags here?" Liam shouts from behind me. I turn back to the group and jog over to grab my bag, which he hands me from the trunk.

"Thanks. Sorry, I was just looking at the view. It's beautiful here. I don't think I've ever actually stayed in a real log cabin before," I say truthfully.

"Really?" Bailey asks, and I shake my head.

"Well, we're happy to be the ones to pop your log cabin cherry!" Damon says excitedly.

"Ew, Damon. Why do you have to phrase it like that?" Charlene groans.

"What? It's just a joke," he defends.

I laugh at their banter as we all lug our bags toward the front door. The inside is even more beautiful than the outside. The front entry leads into an open room with tall ceilings and large wooden support beams. To the left, the living room has a comfy-looking couch and a few armchairs in a semicircle around a huge fireplace centered on the far wall. Behind the couch stands a long wooden dining table with chairs tucked all around it. To the right, the open floor plan leads into a spacious kitchen with beautiful dark oak cabinetry. Perfect for cooking a Thanksgiving dinner.

Charlene and Jenna are the first to sprint up the staircase that ascends just past the front door and leads to the second floor, where all the bedrooms are.

"Bailey and I get dibs on the master suite because I found this place!" Lindsey calls up after them. "But there are three other bedrooms with queen beds, so just grab one of those." She and Bailey start carrying the groceries we brought for tonight into the kitchen. I put my bag down and walk into the living room to look out at the view again. The far-left wall has two large sliding glass doors that lead out onto the back porch. The sunset is going to be *impeccable* from this vantage point later this evening.

"Damon, you get the pull-out couch in the living room," Lindsey says as she starts putting some of our pre-made food platters into the fridge. We stayed up late last night getting the yams and stuffing done so we wouldn't have too much to cook today. All that's left is the turkey and the pie.

"Why do I always get the pull-out couch? Every time we go somewhere, *I'm* on the pull-out couch. Why can't Liam go on the pull-out couch?" Damon whines like a little boy.

"Because I had to sit in the back seat with you and your annoying little habits the whole way here. I've done my due diligence for the weekend," Liam says, pulling out one of the dining room chairs to sit down.

"Well, what about Freya?" Damon asks.

"What about Freya?" I say nervously, turning back to face him.

"She's never been on a trip with us before. I say she has to pay her dues and sleep on the pull-out couch." He's gesturing at me but still addressing Lindsey like he's complaining to Mom.

"Hey! I'm the new meat—don't you wanna wine and dine me? Y'know, give me the best bed so I'll keep coming back?" I ask with a smirk.

"You're not a guest at a hotel that I'm running! You're my friend, and you're a woman. So, I'm treating you with fairness. Isn't that what you guys want? *Equality?*" he says, grasping at straws.

"You're seriously going to make Freya sleep on a lumpy pull-out just because it's her first trip with us? And for the sake of 'equality'? Come on, man. Be a gentleman," Liam counters. Usually, I would've been fine handling the debate on my own. But I have to admit, I get a few butterflies in my stomach when Liam defends me.

"*Ugh*, fine. I'll just suffer from a sore back all week then," Damon huffs. I giggle as I walk over to him near the fireplace and give him a kiss on the cheek.

"Thanks, D," I say with a wink. He smiles at me and squeezes me into a tight side hug.

"Great. It's settled. Now, no more fighting—we're having a fun, family holiday," Bailey calls from the kitchen. He's really taking this 'dad' thing to another level.

"Hey, Linds? How many extra bedrooms did you say were up here?" Charlene yells over the banister from the second-floor loft. The ceilings are so high that they allow for a small balcony that overlooks the first floor.

"Three. Why?" Lindsey asks, pulling a bundle of asparagus out of a grocery bag and placing it on the counter. Damon and I walk over toward the kitchen to better hear what's going on.

"Well, there are only two from what we can tell," Jenna says, now joining Charlene on the landing.

"What? No. The description online said three queens, a king, and a pull-out," Lindsey says, pulling out her phone. Liam, Damon, and I start heading upstairs to look for ourselves. Apparently, sleeping arrangements are going to be harder to figure out than we thought.

"Uh, Lindsey. This says that the third queen *is* the pull-out," Bailey says, looking over her shoulder at the screen.

"No, no, no. It doesn't say that—it says… okay wait. Let me just…" Lindsey trails off, staring at her phone screen as we all reach the top of the stairs and the boys head down the hall to investigate the mysterious third queen bedroom. "Huh. Okay, yeah. I might've made a *little* mistake," she says with a slight cringe.

She and Bailey start making their way upstairs, too. I follow the boys down the hall to scope out the situation and, lo and behold, there are only two other bedrooms in addition to the master suite. Each has just one queen bed inside.

"Well, Jenna and I are in *this* room, so you three can figure out how you want to divide and conquer the other one," Charlene says, gesturing to me, Liam, and Damon before grabbing Jenna's arm and leading her down the hall and back to the first floor.

It isn't until now that I realize the implications of what this means for our sleeping situation, and my stomach drops. Liam and I look at each other for a brief second before I break eye contact and glance at Damon.

"Don't look at me! I've got a pull-out couch with my name on it downstairs. And only my name. 'Cause I'm not sharing," Damon says as he turns and practically sprints toward the stairs.

"Now he's all for the pull-out couch, huh?" Liam says loudly enough for Damon to hear.

"Hey! I always get the pull-out. I thought we already discussed this... good luck, though, bud," Damon calls before disappearing down the stairs.

"All right, it's okay. I'm sure there's an air mattress or something around here somewhere," I say, trying to salvage the situation.

Liam nods. "Yeah, totally. Let's look in the closet—"

"No, there's nothing. The app says there's nothing else. I don't think they want more people staying here than what the beds allow for," Lindsey cuts in. We stand in silence for a second.

"Uh, okay. Well, then Bailey and I will share the king, and the girls can take the queen," Liam suggests, trying to be helpful—but the look on Lindsey's face says otherwise.

"I mean, I don't mind that as long as—" Bailey starts to say, but Lindsey cuts him off.

"Freya, can I speak to you privately for just a second?" she asks with a tight-lipped smile.

"Uh... yeah. Sure," I agree, a little nervous, because I think I already know what she's going to say. I follow her into the bedroom on my right, and she closes the door behind us.

"So, um... I don't want to be that annoying girl who *has* to sleep with her boyfriend wherever they go, but, uh—I'm going to need to be that girl for just this one night because I was really looking forward to it, and I got this house specifically for the king-size bed so that Bailey and I could—"

"Got it! Say no more. You guys can have a beautiful night together in the master suite. Just stop explaining what you plan to do in there because I don't want to know," I say, turning to open the door again.

"Thank you, thank you, thank you! I promise I'll make it up to you," she says, squeezing my shoulders as I reach for the doorknob.

"Don't worry about it. It's my Thanksgiving gift to you," I say, heading back into the hallway.

"You're the best," Lindsey whispers to me, then turns to the boys, who look like they're in the middle of a serious conversation. "Okay, we figured it out!" she announces happily.

Liam looks at us expectantly, and I pat him on the shoulder as I pass by and head toward the staircase.

"Go grab your bag, roomie. We're bunkin' up tonight," I say, then turn around with a sudden thought. "I really hope you don't snore."

***

Liam didn't seem nearly as upset over the news of our sleeping arrangement as I thought he'd be. Actually, he took it really well, which I'm honestly relieved about, because the last thing I needed was for him to bug me all day, complaining about the night to come.

Now, we're all sitting around the long oak dining table, passing plates and serving ourselves portions of the

Thanksgiving meal we made together. Once everyone's settled with full plates in front of them, I clear my throat to get their attention.

"Um, I just wanted to say really quickly before we eat that I'm so grateful I met you all when I did, and I'm even more grateful that you let me sneak my way into all your events and become a part of your friend group. You're honestly the most genuine friends I've ever had, and I really appreciate all of you so much. Even Liam," I add, sending him a teasing wink from across the table.

"Awww, Freya! We're so happy you moved here. You are now a permanent part of our little group," Charlene says with a smile.

"Hell yeah! You're the best, Freya," Damon shouts.

"We're grateful for you, too," Jenna chimes in.

"Love you, Frey," Lindsey adds.

"I'm just thankful that you convinced this one to go out with me," Bailey says from the head of the table, pointing to Lindsey on his left. She blushes a little.

Grinning from ear to ear at everyone's comments, I glance across the table and meet Liam's eyes. He silently reaches for his wine glass and lifts it over the center of the table.

"To Freya," he says.

We raise our glasses and clink them together, everyone echoing Liam's toast.

"Thank you, guys. Happy Thanksgiving!" I say.

There's a chorus of "Happy Thanksgivings," and then we all dig in.

Chapter 11

Dinner is delicious. And the night is easy. We all laugh and swap stories from the week, and no one accuses anyone of not spending enough time with their family, or making poor career choices, or running away from their life. I even convince Liam to dance with all of us again after dinner when we play a Harry Connick Jr. vinyl on the record player in the living room.

Everything is going swimmingly.

That is, until my mother calls me.

She's been trying to get in touch all day. So has my dad, for that matter. I feel like if I ignore the call one more time, I'll be sentenced to an eternity in daughter hell with no hope of escaping my fiery demise or ever redeeming myself in my parents' eyes. So, I excuse myself from the game of

Pictionary we're in the middle of and head out to the back porch as I answer the phone.

"Hi Mom, Happy Thanksgiving!" I say brightly.

"Happy Thanksgiving, sweetheart. How are you?" Her tone is even and pleasant.

"I'm good! We just had dinner, and now we're sharing some pumpkin pie and playing a game. This Airbnb is incredible. It's a cute log cabin right on a lake," I say, trying to keep the conversation from drifting toward my absence in New York.

"Oh, well, that sounds very lovely. I take it you've been getting on well with Lindsey's friends?" she asks.

"Yeah. Yeah, I really have." A genuine smile spreads across my face as I glance over my shoulder and see everyone inside laughing around the coffee table.

"That's just wonderful. Are you happy?" she asks.

"Yeah, Mom. I'm very happy," I say.

"Good. Well, we missed you here today. Scott was home for a bit. And Josie and Fred came with the kids. They wanted to say hi to you earlier, but you didn't answer the phone, and they're gone now, so I'm afraid you missed them," she says with a sigh.

"It's okay. I'll talk to them all at some point, I'm sure. Josie and I were texting earlier. She sent me a cute photo of the kids with the turkey."

"Oh yes, it was probably bigger than both their heads combined." My mom laughs. It's nice to finally have a semi-functional conversation with her. It feels like she's actually supporting me for once.

"So, when are you planning to visit home?"

Oof. Spoke too soon.

"Uh… well, I'm not sure. Soon, maybe?" I say, slightly nervous about her response.

"Maybe? Honey, I haven't seen you in five months. You skipped a major family holiday to spend it with a bunch of strangers, and now you're saying you don't even know when you'll be visiting? You're at least coming home for Christmas, right?"

"Okay, well, first of all, I'm not with a bunch of strangers. I'm with my friends. And second of all—"

"Well, they're *Lindsey's* friends."

I sigh, letting my head drop. "I mean, yes. But they're my friends now, too. I've had five months to get to know them. I think it's safe to say we've gotten pretty close."

"Closer than your friends back home, who you've known practically your whole life?" she asks, doubtful.

"Yes, Mom. Even closer than them. I know this is hard for you to understand, but the people I knew back home weren't really my friends, not in the ways that count. And anyway, my point is that I'm not sure when I'll be home next because—"

"I just don't understand why you think you've built such a better life for yourself over there. You gave up a great job here to take a lower position that pays less. And you're far away from your family and everything you've ever known. We're all just waiting for this phase, or quarter-life crisis, or whatever it is, to pass so you'll come back to the city and be sensible about your future."

This. This is why I've been avoiding her calls.

"Mom. I'm not going through a phase or a crisis. I'm moving forward with my life after getting cheated on by someone I loved and thought I was going to marry. That's a big thing to go through, and I actually think—"

"Well, I just don't get why you wouldn't want to be with your family for Thanksgiving. Or Christmas, from the sound of it," she cuts in. I can practically hear the eye roll through the phone. I take a deep breath.

"You know, you could come out here if you really wanted to see me. Why does it have to be me who makes the trip? It's not fair—"

"Wait, does this have to do with Lindsey? Has she convinced you to move all the way out there just to live with her again? Because if that's the case, you don't have to ruin your life for the sake of a friendship that frankly—"

"Mom, no! This isn't about Lindsey. And can you please stop interrupting me? Just listen. I moved out here because I wanted to. Because I needed a fresh start. Not because I'm in some downward spiral or because I don't love you or Dad. Not because someone forced me to. But because I needed to figure out who I am on my own."

She doesn't interrupt me this time, so I keep going.

"You've never wanted me around my whole life, and now all of a sudden I'm gone, all you care about is that I come back? I really thought you were starting to understand how I felt... but now it's like we're right back where we always are. I'm the disappointment of a daughter, and you're the critical mother."

Silence.

"I'm gonna go," I say. "I'll talk to you soon. I hope you have a nice rest of your evening. Tell Dad I say hi."

I hear her starting to respond, but I hang up and turn off my phone before she can reel me back in. The groveling won't work tonight. I'm just too tired.

I sit down on the top step of the back stairs, placing my head in my hands. The sting of tears prickles behind my eyes.

"Freya?"

I gasp and whip my head around. Liam is standing on the deck, looking down at me. Behind him, the sliding glass door is closed, and the lights inside are off.

I exhale, trying to steady my heartbeat. "How long have you been standing there?"

"I only heard the last bit. I'm sorry. I didn't mean to eavesdrop. I just… you looked upset through the window, and I wanted to make sure you were okay," he says gently.

I turn back toward the lake and watch the way the moon reflects off its surface. I'm a little embarrassed that the whole house probably witnessed my meltdown, but mostly, I'm just too upset to care.

"It's okay. Thank you," I say.

After a moment, I hear footsteps behind me. Then, I feel him sit down beside me on the stoop.

"Want a drink?" he asks, handing me a bottle of wine.

I accept it wordlessly and take a long swig. Cheap Pinot Noir has never tasted so good.

"Thanks. That was definitely needed," I say, handing the bottle back to him. We pass it back and forth for a few minutes in silence before he speaks again.

"If it makes you feel better, we're happy you're here."

I glance over at him. "It does. Thank you. I am, too."

I sigh, turning back to the water. "I just wish my parents understood. All they choose to see is that I left—that I walked away from everything and everyone. But I didn't. I just… I wanted to experience something different before I got stuck in the same place forever."

I don't even realize I'm crying until I feel the wetness on my cheeks. "Sorry. I'm getting into the habit of turning into a blubbering mess around you."

"Hey. Don't apologize. I'm honored to be your shoulder to cry on," he says, reaching behind me to rub my back. "Listen, if this is where you feel like you belong, you don't owe anyone an explanation. You know it—and that's what matters. Don't let guilt convince you to go back to a place that never felt right to begin with."

I sniffle and glance over at him thoughtfully.

"You're really good at giving advice, did you know that?" I ask with a small smile.

"People mention it from time to time. Should've been a therapist, I guess," he says with a shrug.

"Salem would be lost without its greatest tour guide," I tease.

He chuckles, his shoulders bouncing, and pulls me gently into his side. I rest my head on his shoulder and close my eyes. It's the closest we've been since we danced at the Halloween party. It feels nice. Comforting. Safe.

"I hope you stay. In Massachusetts," he says after a quiet beat.

"I hope I stay too," I reply honestly. It's taken a second, but I do feel like I'm starting to belong in Salem. With these people. With my new job. Even with the witches. I don't know why the guilt of choosing to stay still clings to me. It's my life. My decision. And still, that voice in the back of my head—that voice shaped like my mother—always tries to steer me back to New York. Convincing me that I don't belong here. Hopefully, I'll learn to silence that voice soon enough.

"Can I get you anything else? Tea? Shot of whiskey? A lasso on the moon?" he asks, pointing up at the glowing full moon through the tall trees.

I laugh. "Moon would be great, but if that's too much, I'll settle for the whiskey."

"Well, Damon's passed out on the couch, and everyone else has gone to bed. So we can either stay out here and freeze to death, or we can grab the bottle and head upstairs," Liam says.

I let out a big sigh. "I guess we should probably go to bed. It's almost midnight," I say, checking my watch and wiping away the last of my tears. "Thanks for talking to me. You always make me feel a little better."

"Just a little?" he asks, getting up and offering me his hand.

"A little and a half," I tease.

We head back inside, locking the door behind us and grabbing the bottle of whiskey before tiptoeing upstairs so we don't wake Damon. When we get to our shared room, Liam closes the door quietly behind us. We each take a swig from the bottle of Jack Daniels before I grab my pajamas and head into the adjoining bathroom to change.

When I come out, Liam switches with me and heads in next.

A few minutes later, he exits the bathroom, and I'm standing on one side of the bed, awkwardly waiting for him.

"Okay. So… How do you think we should do this?" I ask.

"Well, I was thinking—and hear me out—we get under the blankets. And we go to sleep," he answers sarcastically.

"All right, smart-ass, you know what I mean," I say.

He sits down on the edge of the bed and looks up at me. "I don't know. How do *you* think we should do this?"

"Well, I just feel like we should create some ground rules," I say.

"Ground rules? What, like if I accidentally kick you in the middle of the night, I lose three points?" he teases.

"Liam, oh my God. I'm just trying to make this a little less uncomfortable."

"You find sleeping in the same bed with me uncomfortable?" he teases again.

I scoff. "Well, I'm not jumping for joy over the arrangement, if that's what you mean."

"There's a big gray area between being excited to sleep with me and being disgusted by it." He shrugs.

"Okay, buddy. Listen. I'm not *sleeping with you*—I'm just *sleeping* with you. And against my will, by the way. So yeah, ground rules will help me."

He sighs. "Fine. What are the rules?"

"Well, no touching. No blanket hogging. No snoring. And no crossing the center equator of the bed." I gesture to the invisible line down the middle of the mattress.

Liam rolls his eyes. "How am I supposed to make sure I don't do any of those things while I'm sleeping?"

"If you break one of the rules, you'll be banished to the floor. So you better hope that you don't," I say, lifting the edge of the blanket and hopping into bed.

"Okay, fine. Then I have a rule too," he says as he crawls under the blankets on his side. The bed gets instantly warmer once he's underneath with me. I try not to think about the fact that his firm body is only going to be a few inches away from mine all night.

"And what would that be?"

"You have to sing me a bedtime lullaby. And it has to be the soundtrack to the musical *Cats*, in its entirety. You may begin whenever you're ready," he says in a serious tone, lying down on his pillow and pulling the comforter up to his chin, eyes closed.

"All right. Goodnight, Liam," I say plainly, reaching over to the bedside table to turn off the lamp.

"Goodnight, Freya."

***

I wake up the next morning to the sun shining directly into my eyes. It feels way too early to be awake, and I realize we forgot to close the blinds before going to bed last night. When I try to get up to close them, though, I realize I'm being held in place by a giant arm wrapped around my torso and a warm, hard chest pressed against my back.

I look down to see Liam's hand tucked beneath my waist, his bare arm holding me securely against his firm body. Somehow, in our deep sleep, our legs have intertwined and our bodies have molded together—my small form cradled within his large one. I'm too tired to fight it. And honestly, I *love* the feeling of being tightly squeezed by the giant, warm mountain behind me.

I close my eyes again, ignoring the sunlight on my face, and I easily doze back off within a couple of minutes, feeling safe and warm in Liam's embrace.

When I wake up again, I can tell it's a few hours later by the new placement of the sun through the window. I instantly feel the loss of warmth in the bed, and when I turn around to see if Liam is still there, I'm met with an empty mattress. I hear voices downstairs and realize everyone is probably awake and getting ready to leave.

I can't help but feel a small pang of disappointment that I didn't get to sleep a little longer curled up against the heat of Liam's body. I can't quite identify the feelings that are starting to form in my gut, but all I know is that I like them.

And they all have to do with him.

Chapter 12

December 2024

The end of the year approaches quickly. December has been filled with work, time with friends, and dreading the holidays to come. I decided to go home for Christmas. My flight leaves tomorrow. Honestly, the hassle of arguing with my parents is more emotionally taxing than actually flying home to see them for a few short days. Thankfully, I have the excuse of work to bring me back to Massachusetts promptly on the twenty-sixth.

The only thing getting me through the anxiety and stress of going home for Christmas has been coffee with Liam at the Red Line Café—and the notion that when I leave for New York, I'll be returning to Salem to see him soon after. I try to suppress the feelings that thought gives me as I gaze at Liam from across the table, sipping from his coffee cup in silence. When he catches me staring, he gives me a strange look.

"What?" he asks.

"Nothing," I lie. "I was just thinking… since everyone else is gone for the holidays now and we're the only ones left in town, we could go into Boston tonight and do something fun." I've been wanting to ask him this all morning.

"Oh. Uh, I'd love to. But unfortunately, I have plans tonight," Liam says apologetically.

"What, you have a whole other secret friend group you've never told us about?" I tease.

He laughs. "No, it's December 21st, so tonight's the Winter Solstice. My family always has a big celebration for the Yuletide."

"Oh, right! I forgot you mentioned that last week," I say, recalling his plans.

"Yeah. It's really fun, actually. It's my favorite Pagan holiday of the whole year," he says.

"Why's that?" I ask curiously.

"It's just really joyful. Lifts the spirits, y'know? It's pretty nostalgic for me, as well." He looks like he's picturing a specific memory in his mind.

I smile. "That sounds really nice."

"Yeah, it is." He sits in thoughtful silence for a moment before speaking again. "Would you like to come?"

I'm honestly a little surprised by the invitation. From the way he's described all the holidays they celebrate, I just assumed they were strictly for family.

"Oh. That's really sweet of you to invite me, but I don't want to impose on your—"

"You're not an imposition."

"But don't you want to celebrate with just your family? Have a special evening with them?"

"I always celebrate with just my family. We could use a new face to shake things up a bit. Plus, I want you to come and see how fun a Pagan holiday is. I think you'll have a good time. And it beats spending the night alone in your apartment before you go home tomorrow," he concludes.

I think about it for a second before responding.

"Well, okay. Only if you promise I'm not going to be a distraction or an unwelcome guest," I say, still a little worried I'm intruding.

"I promise. Believe me, they're going to be thrilled when they meet you," he says, taking another sip from his steaming mug.

"Ah. So, I'm guessing you don't bring many girls home to meet the parents?" I tease.

He laughs. "It's definitely been a while."

I see a sad look flash across his face after he speaks. It comes and goes so quickly, though, I question whether it was actually there.

***

When I step out of Liam's car and onto the driveway, I'm struck by the gorgeous home in front of me. The gray house stands three stories tall with a wide front porch and dark blue shutters. A long driveway leads from the dead-end street up to where the house sits on a tall peak overlooking the ocean below. A white fence with a little gate sits to the left of the front door, leading into a large backyard and what I'm sure is a beautiful garden, currently hibernating through the winter, waiting to blossom again in the spring. Hanging from every window and on the front door are ornate holiday wreaths. The sun is just about to set, and the outdoor Christmas lights have already flickered on.

I must've been staring for a while, because Liam is already halfway to the front door when he looks back and whistles to get my attention.

"Are you coming in? Or are you just gonna stand there ogling all night?" he shouts over his shoulder.

I jog to catch up, and we ascend the porch steps together. Before I can even comment on the house, Liam opens the front door and ushers me into the warmth.

"Hello? We're here!" he calls into the foyer as he kicks off his shoes and shrugs off his coat. I follow his lead, and he takes my coat from me, hanging it neatly in the front closet.

Inside, the house is just as beautiful as the outside. Straight ahead is a grand staircase with a polished wooden banister leading up to the second and third floors. The foyer has high ceilings with an elegant chandelier hanging in the center. To the right is a sitting room filled with tall bookshelves and multiple armchairs and sofas, all arranged around an embellished fireplace. Every piece of furniture and decor matches the Colonial style of the house perfectly. To the left is a less formal living room with similarly styled furniture and a large television as its focal point. An archway at the far end leads into a dining room with a beautiful dark wood table. The whole house radiates a cozy, lived-in warmth. All I want to do is curl up in one of the armchairs with a steaming cup of tea and a good book.

Down the hallway to the left of the staircase, I hear voices talking over one another with exuberance. I can't make out the words, but the conversation sounds cheerful and full of life. Liam takes my hand, pulling me gently out of my thoughts as he leads me toward the chatter.

The narrow hallway walls are lined with dozens of framed family photos, ranging from when Liam was a little boy to now. I can't help but scan them as we walk by, hoping I'll get a chance to take a better look later. From what I can glimpse, Liam was an adorable kid.

When we open the door into the kitchen, the voices instantly become louder and more chaotic as their sources are revealed.

Two middle-aged women with long dark hair—nearly identical in the face—sit at a large kitchen table. One is slender while the other is rounder in the middle, and both wear cozy knitted sweaters. As soon as they see us, they abruptly pause their conversation to shout Liam's name, followed by a stream of loving exclamations as they leap up and barrel toward him.

Each pulls him into a long, enthusiastic embrace, kissing his cheeks repeatedly. They're both much shorter than he is, so he has to bend down for each hug. I can't help smiling as they bombard him with overlapping questions—"How was the drive?" "Are you hungry?" "You look cold, want a sweater?" As they shower him with love, I linger sheepishly near the doorway, glancing around the room.

This is a witch's kitchen if I've ever seen one—not that I've seen many. The wooden cabinets are painted a deep purple, and the walls are adorned with eclectic art. Shelves around the room are packed with jars of all shapes and sizes, filled with mysterious herbs and spices. A black cast iron pot steams on the stove, sending a decadent aroma swirling through the air. From the state of the kitchen table, I can't help wondering what they were up to before we interrupted them. The surface is covered in boughs and needles of evergreen, sprigs of holly and mistletoe, and piles of dried orange slices.

"And you must be Freya!" the rounder woman exclaims, pulling me into the warmest, tightest, most tender hug I've ever received. I quickly wrap my arms around her in return. "I'm Liam's mother—it's so nice to meet you!" she says, pulling back with a radiant smile.

"It's so nice to meet you, too, Mrs. Doyle. You have a beautiful home," I reply with a smile.

"Oh, please, call me Paula! And thank you, lovie. This is my sister, Liam's aunt Maureen," she says, gesturing to the other woman still fawning over Liam. At the mention of her name, Maureen turns to us and greets me with the same bubbly energy.

"So good to meet you, Freya!" Maureen says, hugging me in turn.

"You look so lovely tonight," Paula adds.

"Can I get you something to drink? Or a snack? Oh, I can—" Maureen begins, but Liam cuts her off before she can finish.

"Can you two stop harassing Freya and let her get settled? Jeez, we've been here two minutes. You're gonna scare her off."

I wave him off with a smile and turn back to the women. "No, it's okay! Thank you so much for the warm welcome. And thank you for letting me crash your celebration. Liam was kind enough to invite me, I hope that's oka—"

"Oh, of course it is, honey!" Paula interrupts, already ushering us toward the pine-covered table. "Please, sit down. Both of you. I'll get you a drink."

She seats us next to each other while Maureen takes the seat across from us, still beaming.

"We were just about to start our Yule wreaths when you two arrived. Perfect timing, you can join us," Maureen says, reaching for a circle of evergreen she's been weaving.

"Oh wow, that's beautiful. So, you make the wreaths yourselves?" I ask, remembering the ones I saw on the windows and front door when we arrived.

"Yes! It's tradition to make them for the Winter Solstice and hang them around the house. The pine is for healing, the mistletoe for fertility, the holly for protection, and the oranges for vitality and joy," she explains, continuing to wrap the pine around her wreath.

"That's a really lovely tradition. The wreaths are stunning. I can't believe they're homemade," I say, impressed.

"Here you both are," Paula says as she hurries back over with two steaming mugs. The rich, spicy scent wafting from them immediately tells me this is what made the kitchen smell so good.

"Thank you so much, Paula," I say, accepting the mug. "Um, what is it exactly?" I ask, trying not to sound rude or clueless.

Liam jumps in to explain. "It's called Wassail. It's mostly apple cider and ale with cinnamon, cloves, and some other spices. It's a Yuletide tradition. In Old English, I think 'wassail' means 'good health,' right?" He glances at the ladies to confirm.

"That's right! It was also tradition to offer some to the trees and sing to them, to ensure a good harvest for the coming year," Maureen adds, sipping from her own mug.

I nod and take a sip. "Well, it tastes amazing, so I can understand why the trees would want their fair share." The women burst out laughing, and I grin.

"So, Freya," Paula says, "Liam tells us he's been showing you around Salem since you moved this summer. Are you happy with the change?"

"Well, I wasn't too sure at first," I admit. "But Liam has been an amazing tour guide. He's taken me to all the historical spots and helped me see what makes the city special. I have to say, it's really grown on me. I don't think I could picture myself anywhere else now. And making new friends definitely helps." I glance over at Liam, who's already looking at me with a soft smile.

"That's so lovely to hear! Not everyone is so easily charmed by this old town—or by my son, for that matter,"

Paula says with a laugh. "But I'm glad you see what makes it so special." Liam blushes slightly, and I giggle at his mom's teasing.

"It's a great town. And Liam is a great teacher. He's also been telling me all about Wicca and how you raised him in the religion. I find it really fascinating. And honestly, quite beautiful." I flash a shy smile and take another sip.

"Oh, that's wonderful! I'm glad you're embracing it," Paula says, turning her attention to her wreath.

"Took her a second to get past the point of being a total cynic about it. But now she's really come around," Liam teases, smirking.

I swat his shoulder. "Hey! I wasn't that bad."

"You keep telling yourself that," he says, sipping from his mug.

"Oh, hush, Liam!" Paula scolds gently. "I don't blame you, Freya. You're just like Liam's father when he first came here. It can be a little daunting at first, but once you're on board, there's so much wisdom to explore."

No matter how close we get as friends, we still sometimes fall back into our old tendencies of teasing and jabbing, just like when we first met. All in good fun, of course, as Liam would say.

In truth, though I don't feel the need to say it out loud, I'm actually pretty proud of myself for beginning to overcome my prejudices and preconceived notions about Wicca and Paganism. I never thought I'd be capable of that. More than that, I'm starting to find real comfort in the belief system and the idea that there's more to the universe than just physical matter. Maybe there really is some kind of energy that surrounds and connects us all. For the first time in my life, I'm okay not knowing all the answers.

"Since he's been such a good teacher, I assume Liam explained the meaning behind Yule?" Maureen asks, her gaze drifting between the two of us.

I look over at Liam, a little lost for words, because I realize he never actually explained what the holiday was. Although, to be fair, I never asked either. I was too nervous about meeting his whole family to even start thinking about the holiday we were celebrating.

"Uhhh… I was going to let you guys explain it to her," Liam says slowly, as if he hadn't just come up with the excuse a second ago.

"Oh! Well, we've got a lot to catch you up on, then," Paula says, with Maureen nodding beside her. Both of them are giving Liam a stern look, silently scolding him for not teaching me about it beforehand. He puts his hands up in defense, and I let out a laugh before turning back to the two sisters.

"Yule is all about celebrating the return of the sun," Paula begins. "I'm sure you know that today, December 21st, the Winter Solstice, is the shortest day of the year. So every day after this, the days grow longer and longer. Everything we celebrate today revolves around rebirth and preparing for a good year to come. Traditionally, people celebrated Yule over twelve days, with the Solstice as the first. Throughout the holiday, they'd give offerings to the gods of nature and pray for a good harvest in the coming year."

"Like giving Wassail to the trees," I say, recalling Maureen's story from earlier.

"Exactly," Paula says.

I contemplate what she said for a moment, and questions start forming in my mind. "So, how do people celebrate Yule now? I'm guessing most aren't praying for a good harvest," I ask with a chuckle.

Paula laughs. "In any way they choose! Our family likes to celebrate on the day of the Solstice. We drink Wassail and have sweet treats. Eating rich, fatty foods at this time of year is a good way to ensure the coming year is filled with luck and abundance," she says, lifting her mug.

"Well, that makes me feel better about all the Christmas cookies I've been snacking on," I say with a giggle.

"Yes, me too!" Paula laughs.

"We also decorate the house with evergreens, and later we'll light the Yule log to celebrate the sun's return to the sky," Maureen adds, gesturing outside toward the backyard.

Liam finally chimes in, "Like a lot of the other holidays I've explained to you, it's all centered around nature. We're celebrating the cycles of life, showing gratitude for the year that passed, and inviting the new one to start. Traditionally, people prayed for healthy crops or fertile animals. But you can manifest abundance in any area of your life." As he finishes, he reaches for one of the evergreen boughs and some mistletoe.

"It sounds like a really beautiful way to celebrate the holidays. I had no idea so many Christmas traditions were taken from Pagan ones," I add, remembering a conversation Liam and I had months ago. "It's a little sad that most people don't know where the traditions come from."

"We like to think of them as being borrowed rather than taken," Maureen notes. "And honestly, it's okay that most people don't know. The important thing is that the traditions stay alive, in one form or another. As long as people are happy when they celebrate, their good intentions will follow with them," she adds as she continues weaving her wreath, now adding holly and oranges. Her explanation makes complete sense. Before I can ask anything else, Liam starts handing me some pine from the table.

"Here, I'll show you how to weave a wreath, and you can take it home to hang in your apartment."

I smile as he walks me through the steps, and we begin weaving the wreath together. Our fingers touch every so often as we twist the pine with the other plants. Each time they graze, I feel that familiar electric pulse run up my arm and shiver back down my spine.

I get so lost in the intricacy of the weaving and the chatter from the two sisters across the table that I don't even realize when we finish the wreath. It honestly looks much better than I thought it would.

"Wow, this is gorgeous. Did we really just make that?" I ask, a little shocked.

"We really did," Liam says, a smirk on his face.

Maureen and Paula laugh at my amazement, and I chuckle along with them.

"Now you can hang it on your door and it'll bring you good health and abundance in the new year," Paula says, looking at me with a kind smile.

I realize, in that moment, that I don't think my mother has ever smiled at me the way Paula is smiling at me right now. It almost brings a tear to my eye, but I blink it away quickly and suppress the feeling before it can rear its ugly head. *Not the time or place, Freya.*

My thoughts are interrupted when the back door swings open loudly and two large men come traipsing into the kitchen, bundled in giant coats and warm hats. Their conversation stops mid-sentence when they see Liam and me at the table.

"Liam! My boy, I didn't know ya had arrived!" one of the men says. I notice his thick Irish accent right away. Coupled with the black hair, I realize this must be Liam's father.

"We wouldn't have gone on such a long walk if we knew you were here," the other man says, removing his hat to reveal a full head of bright red hair. Liam rises from the table and walks over to greet them.

"Good to see you, Dad," he says, his voice muffled in his father's shoulder as they hug. When they break apart, he turns to the other man and gives him an equally big embrace. "You too, Uncle Wells."

"You boys need to sit down and have a cup of Wassail before you freeze your behinds off!" Paula says, getting up to pour them each a mug of the golden liquid.

"Guys, this is my friend Freya. She's joining us today to celebrate. Freya, this is my Uncle Wells and my father, Cadmun," Liam says, settling back into his seat beside me. I stand and start to extend my hand, but Cadmun pulls me into a giant embrace instead. At this point, I should've expected that and just gone straight for the hug.

"Very good to meet ya, lass! Liam here's told us quite a bit about ya. I was wonderin' when he was going to bring ya 'round," he says, finally letting me go.

"It's really nice to meet you, too. I'm so happy I could come celebrate with you all tonight," I say, moving to greet Wells, who also pulls me into a warm hug.

"You know, you're much prettier than he described you," Wells says, gesturing at Liam as he takes a seat at the head of the table. My eyebrows lift, and I whip my head around to see Liam blushing a deep red.

"You tellin' people I'm pretty?" I tease, sitting back down in my chair.

"No. I am not. He's just lying to get attention," Liam says firmly, trying to salvage his pride.

"Oh, please. You were practically—" Cadmun begins, but Liam cuts him off.

"Okay, okay. We get the picture," he says, clearly trying to shut down the conversation before it goes any further. Paula hands the men two steaming mugs of Wassail, and they accept them gratefully. The mugs look like doll accessories in their giant hands.

"Cadmun. That's such a unique name. I assume it's Irish?" I ask, trying to steer the conversation away from Liam's embarrassment.

"Oh, thank ya! Traditionally, it's actually Welsh. I think my mother just liked the sound of it, though. It means 'warrior,'" Cadmun says, taking a sip from his mug. "Liam's got it as a middle name, as well."

"Liam Cadmun Doyle. That's one hell of a Celtic name," I say with a little laugh.

"Aye, yes. A strong Celtic name!" Cadmun agrees.

"Where in Ireland are you from?" I ask.

"Wexford. It's on the southeastern coastline. The Doyles go back for generations in that part of Ireland. It's a very special place," he says, a far-off look in his eyes.

"Why did you leave?" I ask gently.

"Well, the short answer is I came to Boston for a trip when I was twenty-one, and I fell in love with an American girl. Never went back," Cadmun says, looking at Paula with a fond smile. He reaches across the table to take her hand. "Salem reminds me of Wexford in some ways. Seaport town, right on the water, lots of history, pain-in-the-arse locals," he adds with a booming laugh. "Never hold yourself back from chasing love. It's the one thing worth fighting for in this life," he says, looking directly at me.

If someone had told me that even just a month or two ago, I don't think I would've agreed with them. But tonight, for some reason, I'm inclined to believe him. "I'm happy it all worked out for you both," I say with a smile.

"So am I," Paula adds with a little smirk. Cadmun kisses the back of her hand before leaning back in his chair with his mug.

"It's not easy falling in love with a witch, y'know. Wells can attest to that, too, though he had the advantage of growing up here, so he understood the culture a bit more. I came into it completely blind. And Paula's mother was *not* the biggest fan of me being a Catholic. Don't know how I survived the first few months of courtship," he says, making exaggerated gestures.

"Don't know how I survived it either," Paula adds with a scoff.

"But everything always works out the way it's supposed to. Paula taught me everything she knew, and then we taught our son together. And now, I get to celebrate the Winter Solstice with my family every year." Cadmun raises his mug to the center of the table.

"Here, here!" Wells says, clinking his mug against Cadmun's. They both take a big gulp, and the women laugh at their display.

I can't help but laugh along. Their love story is definitely one to be proud of.

"You three better go out and get the Yule log started! It's not going to burn itself, now is it?" Paula says sternly, pointing at the men.

Liam chuckles and starts to get up with his dad and uncle. "We've got it, don't worry. Freya, you can stay with the girls. I'm sure they have many things they want to talk to you about," he teases. I laugh and stay seated as the three of them head out the back door.

"Freya, why don't you come with me and we'll hang this wreath up in the library?" Paula says, picking up the wreath she made and heading into the hallway. I follow her into the room with all the bookshelves and help her hang the wreath above the fireplace.

On our way back toward the kitchen, I pause to look at some of the photos on the wall again, this time getting a better glimpse. Paula joins me, standing to my right as we both gaze at the pictures.

"He was such a cute kid," I say, pointing to a photo of Liam in a big coat, sitting alone on a park bench wearing a birthday hat. He couldn't have been more than ten.

"That was his eighth birthday party… He was really sad that day, actually." She looks at the photo intently.

"Why?" I ask, confused. He's smiling from ear to ear in the picture. It's hard to believe he was anything but happy at that moment.

"We had planned a big party for him with all his classmates. He wanted to go to the Pirate Museum in town. But only a handful of kids showed up," Paula says with a sad smile. "I took the photo outside the museum while we were waiting for everyone to meet us. Honestly, I'm not really sure why I keep it hung up. Though to your point, he was a very cute kid."

Her story makes my chest twist with pain.

"That's awful," I say, a little lost for words.

"For some reason, he had a hard time making friends in school. He has a hard time making friends now, actually. He's got a tough exterior, doesn't let a lot of people in. I'm sure you know that, though," she says, glancing at me with a little smile.

I chuckle softly. "It was slow going at first. But now, he's one of the best friends I've ever had," I say, returning her smile.

"That's my Liam. He just gets scared that if he lets someone get too close, they'll hurt him. He's always been like that. Don't know why. It's not like me or Cadmun, we're friendly with everyone we meet." She laughs a little, and I chuckle along with her. Another thing that Liam and I have in common.

There are a few seconds of silence before Paula speaks again.

"He likes you. I can tell," she says, gently bumping my hip with her own. I turn to face her, my eyebrows knit slightly in surprise.

"He's had a hard year. And I don't think I've seen him smile this much in a long time. You bring out a nice side in him, and I hope you continue to come around, Freya."

Her words render me speechless for a moment.

"Oh, I uh—that's really kind of you. I… I don't know what to say." My mind is reeling. I'm sure my response is nowhere near adequate.

"You don't have to say anything. I'm just happy you were able to come tonight," she says kindly, and I smile.

"So am I. Thank you again for having me," I say sincerely, a smile tugging at my lips.

Paula pulls me into another warm hug, and I realize I don't want her to let go.

We head back into the kitchen and pour ourselves fresh cups of Wassail, then sit back down at the table with Maureen. I think back to something Paula mentioned in the hall. It's the second time someone's said Liam's had a bad year. Before I can begin to wonder what that means, Maureen draws me back to the present by asking about my job.

I tell them about being a journalist, about growing up in Manhattan, and going to Columbia. I stick to the happy parts and omit the domineering parents, the cheating boyfriend, the fake friends, and the constant feeling of not belonging. Apparently, without all the drama, my story doesn't take long to tell.

I'm saved by the bell when Liam opens the back door to let us know the fire is ready. Just in time, too—Paula had just asked about my parents, and I'm not quite ready to open that door. They still think I come from a pleasant home, and I want them to keep thinking that for as long as possible.

I grab my coat and shoes from the front hall and head out the back door, joining Liam, Cadmun, and Wells by the giant fire they've built. I sit next to Liam on one of the log benches around the fire pit. Maureen and Paula follow with a tray of sweet snacks and more Wassail for everyone. They sit on the opposite bench and pass around desserts that look too good to turn down.

We eat, drink, and bask in the fire's warmth. Conversation flows, laughter fills the air, and merriment spreads. Eventually, Liam turns to me and explains a meditation ritual he and his family do together every year, centered around the Yule log. He tells me it's a time to reflect on the past year, giving thanks for the good moments, letting go of the bad ones, and remembering the lessons learned. Then, he says, you envision what you want the next year to look like, set intentions to reach those goals, and embrace the cleansing energy the Solstice brings to release anything that no longer serves you.

As silence falls over us and we all close our eyes to focus inward, I comb through the memories of the past year, taking stock of the hardships, the good times, and the personal growth that has shaped me into the person I am today. I smile a little, realizing that I have Liam to thank for most of that growth. It's no surprise to me that when I envision the year ahead, I picture us together, exactly as we are. But not only that, I see all our friends with us as well. I see myself thriving in an independent life I have created for myself. Above all, I see happiness. My happiness.

When I open my eyes, I glance over at Liam on my left, his eyes still closed, and I can't help but admire his beautiful profile.

After our group ritual, Cadmun grabs his fiddle and Wells his acoustic guitar, and they begin to play some Celtic tunes. It reminds me of the nights at O'Neill's, when we'd listen to the band play Irish music late into the night. I sing along to the songs I know and listen happily as Liam and his family sing the ones I don't.

Once they're warmed up, the music shifts into a fast jig. Liam rises from his spot beside me and extends his hand.

"Dancing happens to be another Yule tradition. And I happen to know that you really enjoy dancing," he says with a teasing smirk.

I smile, take his hand, and let him pull me up, following him to the open space behind the benches.

He draws me into a loose frame, his right hand on my lower back, his left gripping mine. I place my left hand on his shoulder, and before I can find my footing, he leads us into a quick dance around the fire. I follow his steps, keeping my eyes on his to avoid getting dizzy. Our bodies sway to the rhythm, moving rapidly. It almost feels like I'm flying as Liam spins us with confidence, his grip steady, his eyes promising me I won't fall.

Paula and Maureen are clapping along to the music as we continue to skip around the circle, and I can't help but start to laugh. This has to be one of the most exhilarating feelings I've ever felt. We're moving so quickly through the cold December air, and I'm so mesmerized by Liam's green orbs that I accidentally step on his toes, which causes him to lose his balance. He stumbles, and we both go down. Fast.

I don't even register the fall until I'm flat on top of him, my cheek pressed against his chest.

We're both laughing too hard to be embarrassed. My stomach feels like it's in stitches, and I have tears streaming down my face from the giggles. I try to get up but fail, so I roll off to the side and lie on the ground until Liam stands and pulls me up.

"You okay?" he asks, still chuckling as he brushes dirt and grass off my back.

"I'm good. That was so much fun!" I say, breathless and smiling.

"How about we slow it down for you this time?" Wells says with a wink. I hadn't even noticed they'd stopped playing, but the music starts up again just as quickly.

"Mom, Aunt Maureen, you guys have to dance too!" Liam says, holding out his hands. After some protest, they give in and rise to join us. We all take hands and skip around the fire, laughing, spinning, and cheering until the women collapse back onto the benches.

Cadmun and Wells slow the music even more. They're clearly getting tired, but they insist we keep dancing.

Liam pulls me into a close hold again, our hands finding their familiar places. I'm instantly brought back to the Halloween party, to our first dance.

We sway slowly. Just like that night.

I lay my cheek on his shoulder, and everything feels good. Our bodies mold together naturally, turning slowly around our shared center. The feeling I had back then returns, but this time, I'm not surprised by it. I expected it.

Instead of running from it, I embrace it wholeheartedly. It's warm, comforting, and impossible to ignore. I want it to consume me completely, to fill every inch of me. I still don't know what the feeling is, exactly. But I don't care. I just know I never want it to go away.

Eventually, Cadmun and Wells get too tired to play, and Maureen and Paula get too tired to listen. They retreat inside for a nightcap before bed, but not before giving Liam and me warm hugs, exchanging "Happy Solstices," and "Good nights," and "Sleep wells," and "It was so lovely to meet yous."

Finally, Liam and I sit back down on the bench, basking in the dying warmth of the fire's embers. It's the first moment we've been alone since we arrived earlier today, and I'm a little excited to have him to myself again. After a few seconds of silence, he turns to look at me and scoots closer until our thighs are touching and there's no space between us.

"I really love your family," I say with a smile.

"They definitely loved you, too. I've never seen them so excited about someone I brought home before," he says, nudging my shoulder.

"Not even Damon?" I ask, feigning shock.

"Not even Damon. Can you believe that?" he replies, playing along.

I laugh and look down at my feet.

"Seriously, though, I've never felt this happy celebrating a holiday. Not even with my own family," I say.

"You don't like the holidays?" he asks.

"Not usually. They come with a lot of stress, so I always try to just rush through this time of year. I guess it's nice to experience them when there's actual joy and merriment involved," I say with a small smile.

"Well, I think I can speak for everyone when I say we're all really happy to have you here this year. I don't think we've ever had that much fun either, honestly," he says. "And I'm sorry that's how you see this time of year. I wish I could take all your stress and throw it into the ocean so you didn't have to deal with it anymore."

I chuckle. "Thanks for the sentiment. That's very kind of you," I say. "And thank you for inviting me tonight. Learning about the holiday and participating in your traditions has been amazing. I wish I could do this every year."

I glance over at him and smile. Our gazes meet, and it looks like he's trying to tell me something with his eyes, but once again, just like at the Halloween party, I can't understand the message. He finally breaks our eye contact and starts digging into his jacket pocket.

"I almost forgot. I have a gift for you," he says, and I'm a little taken aback.

"What? I didn't know we were doing gifts! You told me not to bring anything." Now I'm upset that I didn't get him something despite his instructions.

"It's okay. I don't need anything. That's why I didn't tell you I was getting you something," he says, handing me a small red box.

I look at it for a couple of seconds in silence before glancing back up at him. "Thank you, Liam. Now I feel terrible that I—"

"Ah ah! I don't want to hear it. Just open the gift." He cuts me off with a raised pointer finger before I can start lamenting about how sorry I am that I didn't get him anything. First, he doesn't tell me we're doing gifts, and now he won't even let me apologize? *What a jackass.*

"Okay, okay," I say with a chuckle, lifting the small flat lid off the box. My breath catches when I see what's inside.

The necklace lies on a square piece of cotton. It has a delicate gold chain and a small pink crystal clasped in golden claws. It's so gorgeous, I could cry.

In fact, I do cry. I guess I can't help it.

"It's rose quartz. It's supposed to be a powerful tool for releasing emotional trauma and finding a true state of happiness and inner peace. I know you say you're okay most of the time. And I believe you. But just in case you might need a little help on your journey to find love and happiness, I thought this couldn't hurt. Plus, I think it'll bring out your eyes," he says, refusing to meet my gaze. He shrugs his shoulders like he didn't just say the most profoundly romantic thing anyone has ever said to me.

I look back down at the box and the necklace.

"I don't even know what to say. Thank you, Liam. Really, I mean it. Thank you." I look back up, tears still rimming my eyes.

"I know you mean it. And you're welcome." He takes the necklace out of the box and motions for me to turn around so he can put it on.

I feel him gently move my hair out of the way and loop the chain around my neck, fastening the clasp at the back. I look down at the stone resting on my chest and gingerly take it between my fingers, admiring its beauty.

I'm not entirely sure where I get the courage to do what I do next. Maybe it was what Paula told me earlier in the hallway. Or the way Liam held me while we danced. Or the fact that he just gave me the most beautiful necklace I've ever seen.

Whatever the reason, I turn back around to face him, look into his eyes for a moment, and then I lean in and press my lips to his.

My hand instinctively moves to his cheek as his arms wrap around my waist and pull me closer on instinct. Our lips move together in sync. His are as soft as I imagined, maybe even softer. After a minute or two, I feel his tongue brush against my lips, asking for permission. I part my lips slightly and let him in.

We deepen the kiss, our tongues dancing together, neither trying to dominate. That feeling I had when we were dancing returns with a vengeance, sweeping through my stomach and chest, creating a tingling sensation in my arms and legs. I'm addicted to it. I wish I could bottle it up and take it home with me to use whenever I needed a hit.

After what feels like only a few seconds—but I'm sure it was much longer—Liam pulls his lips from mine, and suddenly I feel a thousand times colder than before. He stands up from where he was sitting next to me.

"I, uh... I'm sorry, Freya—I can't. I, I'm..." he stammers, unable to look at me or get his thoughts together. He starts pacing the lawn.

"I'm so sorry," I say, realizing I just jumped him without even asking if I could kiss him. I'm in the middle of mentally kicking myself for ignoring the basic tenets of consent when Liam interrupts my thoughts.

"Don't apologize. I'm the one who's sorry," he says, stopping in his tracks but still not looking at me. I rise from the bench.

"It's okay. I shouldn't have done that. It was a mista—"

"Don't say that." He finally meets my eyes. It looks like there are tears gathering near his bottom lashes, though it could just be the firelight.

"Is everything okay, Lia—"

"I think you should go, Freya." He drops his gaze again.

"I, um—what?" I ask, confused.

"I'll call you a cab to bring you home so you don't have to walk in the dark. Thank you for coming tonight, but I'm just getting a little tired now, and I think I'm going to go to bed," Liam says, quickly and evenly.

His words confuse me even more, and honestly, they hurt, especially since he was supposed to drive me home. But what stings most is that he still won't look at me.

"Liam, I know something is wrong. You can tell me wha—"

"No. It's okay. Everything is fine. I'm just tired." He interrupts me again.

I know he's lying, but he's being so insistent, I don't want to push him and make him uncomfortable.

"Okay," I say after a beat of silence. "I'll go."

He stares at the dying fire for a few moments before nodding once and turning to walk toward the house. But not before stopping in front of me first and finally looking into my eyes one last time.

"You can hang out in the living room for as long as you need," he says, implying he isn't even going to wait with me for the cab. That hurts even more.

After a second, his eyes flick down to my lips, then to the necklace hanging around my neck.

He reaches out and lightly grazes the stone. "It really does look beautiful on you, Freya." He stares at it for another second, then turns on his heel and walks straight to the back door, without looking back once.

The feeling of abandonment twists deep in my gut.

I leave in a cab fifteen minutes later. I'm not entirely sure what to think. But I know something has changed.

And I don't like it one bit.

Chapter 13

Christmas is here, and somehow, my family drama is the last thing on my mind. Liam has completely taken over my brain. I guess the secret to overcoming familial stress is to kiss one of your best friends. Who would've thought? If I had known, I might've done it years ago. Although… maybe not. Because the stress of thinking about what happened with Liam has somehow surpassed the usual amount of stress I carry about my family.

Well, maybe not entirely surpassed. I do have one moment of panic on the plane when I realize this is the first time I'm coming home since I left six months ago. My mind drifts to all the fights that are likely in my future, especially with my mother.

But then I look down at the rose quartz necklace resting against my chest. I couldn't bring myself to take it off, even after everything that happened. I think back to what Liam told me about how the stone can help with releasing emotional trauma and finding inner peace. I pray it will help me through the weekend.

When I arrive on Christmas Eve, my mother actually seems excited to have me home. I keep waiting for the other shoe to drop and for her to start berating me about moving back to New York. But she never does. Instead, she gets me a drink and fills me in on the latest gossip from her friend circles. Still, I'm left on edge.

It's funny how being back in your childhood home can catapult you straight into feeling like a child again. As if every lesson I've learned about myself and the world just evaporates, and I never actually grew up.

After everything I've learned from Liam, I know I should be better. I should approach this weekend with a positive outlook, because I know now that my mindset could make a huge difference in the outcome of the holiday. But somehow, that feels more impossible than ever. Especially after how Liam and I ended things the other night.

How am I supposed to put all my hope in Magick if I'm currently losing hope in the person who taught it to me? He hasn't answered any of my calls or texts since that night. I got the hint pretty quickly that he doesn't want to hear from me.

So instead of making an effort, I spend most of the holiday sulking around the house, half-listening to conversations about my brother-in-law Fred's promotion, my niece and nephew's good grades, or my mom's new Pilates routine.

On Christmas morning, we exchange gifts, and I feel like a stranger at a party where only close friends are invited. I watch Josie and Scott toss around inside jokes I've never been privy to. My dad is actually present with the family, his Bluetooth and emails forgotten, as he plays with Josie's kids like a real grandfather would. My mom smiles sweetly as she sits by the tree, dispersing gifts with a cup of coffee in her hand.

And nobody is fighting. Or yelling. Or storming out of the room in a fit of anger.

Suddenly, I realize something.

Maybe my family members aren't the monsters I've made them out to be in my head. Maybe they're just a normal family who have normal gatherings and want to be in each other's lives because they love each other. Not because their parents are forcing them to be there, or because the generational wealth draws them back, but because they choose to be together. Sure, they may have flaws. They may live in a bubble. But that doesn't make them bad people.

Maybe they really *are* the perfect family. And I'm not a part of that. Not because they didn't want me to be, but because I pulled away. I isolated myself.

Why? Because I felt like I was different?

No. Because, deep down, I thought I was better than them. I judged them.

Just like I had judged Liam.

Maybe *I'm* the monster.

I slowly stand up from my spot on the couch and head into the kitchen for more coffee. The laughter and chatter from the living room slowly dull as I move farther away. I top off my mug from the coffee pot and lean against the counter, looking at the shelf to the right of the coffee station, which always showcases about a half dozen picture frames.

Each frame holds a family photo. One of everyone, minus me, together at Disney World. One of Josie and Scott dressed nicely, holding drinks at what looks like a party, possibly Easter, judging by the decorations in the back. One of my parents, smiling wildly into the camera, arms around each other on the deck of a boat sailing down the Hudson. The perfect family. *All without me.*

I scan the rest of the photos, searching for one with me in it. I spot one near the back—an old picture taken over ten years ago at my high school graduation. But that's it.

Not really surprising, though. I can't remember the last time I stood for a photo with my family.

I feel that familiar sadness creep in, the one I always feel when I see my family together and I'm not included. But the reality is, I've always been included. They invited me to every single event captured in these pictures. And I refused to come. Because I thought they didn't actually want me.

But I'm realizing now… that might not be true. Maybe it's always been me, projecting that belief onto them.

In truth, none of them ever claimed the family was perfect without me. That was my own idea.

I hear footsteps coming up beside me, and someone stops and stands to my left. I don't have to turn to know it's my dad, joining me to gaze at the family photos.

"These are some nice pictures," I say without turning to face him.

"Yes. Would've been nicer with you in some of them," he responds solemnly. I glance at him, but he doesn't look over, so I turn back to the shelf.

We stand in silence for a moment before he speaks again.

"I'm glad you came home, Freya."

I glance over again, and this time he turns to meet my gaze, a soft smile on his face.

"Me too, Dad," I say genuinely.

Another beat of silence.

"Your mom and I know you're happy in Salem. And we're happy that you're happy." He's turned back to face the photos again, but I keep my eyes on him.

"Really?" I ask, surprised.

"I know it doesn't always seem that way, especially with your mother. But yes, really." He nods a bit. "It's just not the life we pictured for you. So it took some time for us to adjust. But I realized pretty soon after you left that the life we wanted for you wasn't the one you were meant to live. Your mom knows that now, too. I know she came off harsh on the phone on Thanksgiving, but it's only because she misses you. We both do."

"I just always thought you guys didn't support me because you wanted me to be someone different. More like you." The words slip out before I can stop them. The honest truth.

Finally, he turns to look at me again. "I'm sorry if that's ever how we made you feel. How *I* made you feel. That was never my intention." He sighs and shifts his whole body to face me. "I think we just sensed that you always wanted different things. And rather than encourage that, we tried to make you like us. That wasn't right. Maybe if we hadn't done that, you would've wanted to stick around a little more."

I look at him sadly, still a little shocked we're having this conversation, but grateful that we are. It's the unspoken reality we've all been living in.

I sigh and look down at my feet before replying. "It wasn't all you guys. I isolated myself. I think I always felt like an outsider, and the four of you just clicked so well. I painted this whole picture that you didn't want me, or that you didn't love me as much. And that wasn't fair at all. I'm sorry, Dad."

Sure, they've hurt me in ways. But I'm not blameless.

He shakes his head. "It's not your job as the kid to be sorry. You should never have been made to feel that way." He pulls me into his side, and I quickly put my mug down on the counter, wrapping my arms around him.

"I think it took you leaving for us to realize how you truly felt. And I'm sorry it took that long," he says into my hair. Tears prick at my eyes, and I nod rapidly, unable to speak for a moment.

"Thanks, Dad," I say into his chest. As we hug, I reach up and grasp the rose quartz hanging from the chain around my neck, silently thanking its power—and Liam, for giving it to me.

***

After my conversation with my dad, I realize it's time to change. It's time to move on from the past and focus on my family for who they are today.

I stay in the kitchen for a few minutes after my dad returns to the living room. Eventually, I follow him back in and take my seat on the couch again. We open the rest of the gifts and stay present with one another. Instead of wallowing in negativity, I shift my mindset to a more positive one and choose to be grateful for the people around me. And it feels way better than I could have imagined.

I actually participate in conversations and laugh along with my siblings' jokes. I don't roll my eyes when my mom brings up the New Year's party she's hosting, and I even find myself asking Scott how his job at Dad's firm is going. I can feel the invisible barrier lifting between me and my family.

Soon, all the gifts are opened, and the kids pass out on top of the ripped wrapping paper as the sun sinks lower into its afternoon glow. Dad, Fred, and Scott leave us to finish up the last parts of our dinner, and I listen to my mom and Josie talk about how special these early Christmases with the kids can be. That's when an idea forms in my head.

I stand and walk over to the cabinet beneath the TV. Opening it, I rummage through its contents, trying to find the item I'm looking for. Finally, I find it.

I take the DVD out of its case, wordlessly pop it into the player, and press play before sitting back down on the couch.

My lips curve into a small smile as the opening credits for *It's a Wonderful Life* flash across the screen.

"Oh! I haven't seen this movie since we were kids," Josie says excitedly once she realizes what I've put on. My mom glances over at me, and I turn to meet her eyes. A small smile spreads across her face, and she looks at me in a way I feel like I haven't seen since I was a child. Then, she stands from her chair and comes to sit next to me on the couch, resting her hand on my knee and giving it a loving squeeze. She knows this is my way of apologizing.

She lets a few minutes pass before leaning in close and whispering in my ear, "We never didn't want you around."

I let the words sink in for a moment before wrapping my arm around her shoulders and pulling her close as a small tear rolls down my cheek. I know this is her way of apologizing, too.

Eventually, Josie joins us on the couch and snuggles her way into Mom's other side. Toward the end of the movie, the boys come back into the living room to watch the rest with us, but not before my dad snaps a quick photo of the three of us together on the couch. As the end credits roll, I look around at my family, all together. And I'm happy.

After so many years of not watching it, I realize I had forgotten the most pivotal lesson of the film: never take your loved ones for granted.

***

Later on, after we finish dinner, Fred goes upstairs to put the kids to bed with Scott's help, and Mom and Dad settle down in the den to watch a Hallmark movie. I find a moment to slip out to the back balcony with a dirty martini I made for myself from my parents' well-stocked bar.

As I slide into one of the patio chairs, my mind drifts to Liam. Somehow, I had managed not to think about him for most of the day, too focused on my family. But now that the day is almost over, the world around me has quieted just enough to let those pesky thoughts back into my head. I wonder what he's doing tonight, how he might be celebrating Christmas with his own family. Maybe they watched *It's a Wonderful Life,* too. I'll have to ask when I'm back. If he'll talk to me, that is.

The balcony door slides open, and I turn to see Josie stepping through the threshold, a dirty martini of her own in hand.

"I see you still have great taste in cocktails," she says with a smirk as she sits down in the chair next to me.

"You were the one who made me my first one at that benefit we hosted here when I was like sixteen, remember?" I say with a chuckle.

"Oh, yah! And Mom yelled at me because she didn't want people thinking she was raising two teenage alcoholics."

We both burst out laughing and clink our glasses together in a toast. Then we're quiet for a minute. And Liam crawls his way back into my thoughts. I must have a certain look on my face, because Josie asks me what's wrong.

"Nothing. I'm fine. Just boy stuff," I say, taking a sip from my glass.

"Really?!" Josie asks, surprised and intrigued. "You're not thinking about getting back together with Jackson, are you? I always thought you could do so much better. Or is this a new guy from Massachusetts?"

I blow some air out of my nose and shake my head. "It is definitely not Jackson," I say firmly. It's nice to hear her back me up on the Jackson front, though.

Josie laughs. "You don't have to tell me if you don't want to. But whoever this guy is, you should talk to him when you get back. It's not good for your brain to be mulling over something as much as you are right now."

"Is it that obvious?" I ask with a little giggle.

"Believe me. As someone who's been there before, I recognize the face," she says, then imitates my contemplative and anxious expression.

"Whatever happened, you've given him some time to figure it out. Now you can talk to him. Men never know what they're feeling at the time they're feeling it. It takes their brain at least a few business days to catch up with their heart."

I laugh at her analysis.

"You know this from Fred, I suppose?" I tease.

"Oh, of course," she says, taking a sip of her martini.

We giggle together like two little kids telling secrets.

Chapter 14

New Year's Eve

If there are two things I've learned since coming back to Salem after Christmas, it's that the city looks absolutely gorgeous under a blanket of freshly fallen snow. And I am head-over-heels, scream-it-from-the-rooftops, pick-out-a-white-dress, sing-Taylor-Swift-at-the-top-of-your-lungs *in love* with Liam Cadmun Fucking Doyle.

I nearly threw up on the plane ride back to Boston when I realized it. After replaying every coffee date, every small touch, every teasing joke, every sensual dance, and all the moments in between, it hit me all at once. That fluttery, electric feeling I kept getting anytime he was near? Yeah… it's love.

One thing's for sure: I've been in love with him since Halloween, and I'm a little shocked it took me this long to admit it to myself. Then again, I've been so dead-set against falling in love again that it's not hard to believe I did everything in my power to resist it. Especially for *Liam.* Why did it have to be Liam?

But, who else could it have been?

I'm in love with Liam Doyle. And that's not even my biggest problem.

Because the man I happen to be in love with won't even talk to me.

He didn't even respond to my "Merry Christmas" text, which I sent after that conversation with my sister. I've been back in town for a week, mostly buried in work, and I haven't seen Liam once. Apparently, he's been visiting family, but I'm not convinced that's true.

Lindsey doesn't know about the kiss. Normally, I'd tell her something like that, but this whole thing feels too personal. Too raw. I don't think I should talk about it before I fully understand it myself. Because right now? I don't. Not even a little bit. I really thought I was reading the signs right, that we were feeling the same things. But somehow, I was completely wrong.

All I want is to talk to him. To know what he's feeling. Then maybe I could figure out how to get over these feelings I've suddenly discovered for one of my best friends.

Or worse… I'll have to figure out how to *date* one of my best friends.

That thought is so terrifying, I won't even go near it. After how poorly things ended the last time I was in love, I'm not so confident in my abilities to try it again. And when it all blows up, which it will, I will have lost not only a lover, but a friend as well.

Don't get ahead of yourself. One thing at a time, I tell myself as I unlock the apartment door and step inside.

"Are you going to be ready to go soon?" Lindsey asks the moment I walk in.

"Hi. Nice to see you too. Work was great, thanks for asking. I had a turkey sandwich for lunch," I reply, hanging up my coat and brushing past her into the kitchen in search of a snack.

"Hi, hi, hi. Good day? Great! Are you going to be ready to go soon?" she speeds through the pleasantries, then circles back to her original question, following me into the kitchen.

"Go where?" I ask through a mouthful of leftover chocolate cake from Lindsey's mom's Christmas dessert spread.

"The *party,* dummy! It's New Year's Eve. We're supposed to be at Charlene and Jenna's in thirty minutes!" she says, pointing at the oven clock.

8:03 p.m.

I hadn't even realized how late it was.

"Okay, okay, I'll be ready," I say, throwing up my hands. "Damn, I've never seen you this stressed about being on time."

Within twenty minutes, I'm changed and ready wearing a black Versace cocktail dress and sleek black Louboutin heels. We have five minutes to spare, so we take a quick shot of tequila before heading out. Luckily, Charlene and Jenna live just a short walk away, so there's no need to rush.

"Is everyone going to be there tonight?" I ask, trying not to sound too obvious about the one person I'm hoping will show up.

"Pretty sure! And Damon's bringing a date. I don't know her, but he claims she's his future wife, so we all have to be on our best behavior," Lindsey says, rolling her eyes.

I laugh and promise to play along.

When we arrive, Charlene and Jenna greet us with hugs and usher us toward a makeshift bar—a folding table covered in bottles and red solo cups. A few people I don't know are already mingling and dancing to the music. Damon and Bailey arrive a few minutes later with Damon's mystery date. Her name is Amy, and she's *gorgeous*.

"Nice work," I mouth to Damon with an enthusiastic thumbs up. He blushes and swipes his hand through the air, playfully telling me to cut it out.

Bailey and Lindsey share a sweet kiss, and I exchange hugs with the guys. Eventually, we all settle into a conversation about the holidays, trading stories from the past week.

Time inches by, and as we get closer to midnight, I start to get nervous that Liam isn't coming.

But finally, just after eleven, I see him walk in. He greets Charlene and Jenna with a bottle of wine, then makes his way to the kitchen where we're all gathered.

"There he is!" Damon calls out. "What took you so long, man?"

"Sorry. Lost track of time," Liam says with a shrug.

He's lying, I can tell. And I can't help but wonder if *I'm* the reason he hesitated to come.

"Liam, I want to introduce you to Amy…" Damon says, but I barely hear the rest. Liam greets Amy, then makes his rounds, offering everyone a hug and a "Happy New Year."

When he gets to me, I brace for him to ignore me completely. But he doesn't. He gives me a quick hug and the same generic greeting he gave everyone else.

And he acts like everything is fine. Actually, he acts like we barely know each other. Like we haven't been getting coffee together every week for several months. Like we've never danced together in the way that we have. Like we've never shared some of our deepest thoughts with each other. Like we've never even kissed.

And somehow, that hurts more than if he'd thrown my drink across the room, slapped me in the face, and cursed me out in front of everyone. At least then, I'd know I meant *something* to him. That the kiss meant something.

But he's acting like it didn't. Like that night was just another night. Like I'm just another friend.

And I hate it.

He doesn't speak to me again for most of the night. Doesn't even glance in my direction. I try to ignore it, but eventually, I can't take it anymore. I set my drink down on the counter and walk over to where he's talking with Bailey. I tap him on his shoulder, and he turns. His green eyes are darker than I've ever seen them before. I don't like the feeling I get when he locks them onto mine. It's not how I usually feel when our gazes meet.

"Can I talk to you? Privately," I say, gesturing toward the balcony.

He hesitates, glancing behind me, but then nods and follows me through the crowd to the sliding glass doors. It's freezing out, and I don't have a coat, but I barely notice. My brain is spinning too fast.

I close the door behind us and turn to look at him. He stands with his back to me, gripping the railing and staring down at the alley below.

"How are you?" I ask softly.

"Fine," he says, eyes still fixed downward.

"Really? Because you don't seem fine."

"Freya. Don't. I'm okay."

"Well, I'm not," I say, and that makes him turn to look at me.

"You've been avoiding me since the Solstice, and I want to know why."

He exhales slowly. "I'm not avoiding you—"

"Yes, you are!" I cut in, my voice raises a bit. "You can't ghost me for a week and treat me like some acquaintance you barely know, and then claim that you're not avoiding me. And you definitely can't do that after I *kissed* you. It's not fair."

"Why isn't it fair? It was just a kiss. Don't act like it was something bigger than that," he snaps.

I wasn't expecting that. "Is that really how you feel?"

He doesn't answer. His eyes drop to his feet.

"Because if that's how you feel, then fine. We can go back inside and never talk about it again. We can go back to ignoring each other and pretending we don't care. Is that what you want?"

"No. Of course it's not what I want," he says, looking up and locking eyes with me again.

"Then *what's* the problem? We were good before. Great, even. And then I kissed you, and everything changed. Do you think it was a mistake? Do you not like me that way? Because if you don't, just *tell* me. I can take it. But I can't take this, being shut out, wondering what the hell you're feeling. It's agonizing."

"No, it's not that: I just—I…" He stumbles over the words.

"Then why are you pushing me away?" I yell.

"I can't—Freya, I *can't* do this right now. Please just—"

"No! That's not good enough. I deserve a reason. I can't keep living in this limbo, not knowing where we stand." I'm getting frustrated.

Inside, I hear the New Year's countdown starting.

"I know, okay? I'm sorry I haven't been talking to you. But I just can't—"

"Bullshit! It's not that you *can't,* it's that you *won't.* Just tell me why. I can take it, I'm a strong girl. Why won't you talk to—"

"Because the last girl I fell in love with is *dead* now because of me! So forgive me if I don't want to repeat that pattern again."

Inside, everyone erupts into cheers. Whistles blow. Firecrackers pop. People yell "Happy New Year!" from balconies and open windows. But I'm frozen in place, the January air biting at my bare skin, completely stunned.

Liam's words hang in the air. I try to comprehend them, but my brain is short-circuiting from all the information I just learned in one simple sentence.

"I… I didn't know."

"Yeah. Of course you didn't. I didn't tell you," he mutters sharply, turning back toward the railing.

He's angry. And I get it. I pushed him too hard.

I honestly can't think of what to say next. Do I apologize? Do I curse him out for not telling me this giant secret he's obviously been holding onto for who knows how long? Do I kiss him, because he basically just told me he loved me?

I don't do any of those things.

Instead, I stand there in complete stillness and silence, trying to wrap my head around what just happened.

Before I can even begin to process what I'm feeling, Liam turns back around to face me. Our eyes meet for a few lingering seconds before he starts walking toward the sliding glass door.

I know then that the conversation is over.

So I let him go without a word and watch as he steps back inside. He walks straight to the front door, grabs his coat, and leaves without saying goodbye to anyone. Somehow, no one notices.

I stay where I am, peering into the apartment through the glass. Everyone is hugging and clinking glasses, shouting "Happy New Year!" and laughing with joy. But I don't feel like celebrating.

I turn back toward the alleyway and the bare brick of the building across from us. I glance down to the left and spot a figure walking away on the sidewalk just outside the building. He's instantly recognizable with his long coat and even longer legs.

"Happy New Year, Liam," I whisper, watching him disappear under the orange glow of the streetlamps.

Chapter 15

New Year's Day

After a few more minutes of freezing my ass off on the balcony, I finally decide to head back inside and face my friends. I'm sorting through the avalanche of emotions swirling around in my head, but the strongest, by far, is confusion.

Confused that Liam never told me, even though he's had so many chances over the past few months.

Confused because I still don't totally understand how he feels about me, though he did tell me he loves me, in a weird, twisted way.

Confused that no one, not even Lindsey, ever hinted at the fact that this tragedy happened in his life. And I *know* they all knew. Aside from being his friends, the way they kept saying he'd had a rough year or telling me to go easy on him kind of gave it away.

But mostly, I'm confused by what he said about it being his fault. Why would it have been his fault?

All of these thoughts are jumbled together, pounding at my brain until I feel an actual headache forming. I need to talk to Lindsey. Now.

I find her and Bailey tucked into a corner of the living room, smiling and speaking in low tones, cozy as ever. Normally, I'd think it was cute. But I have other things on my mind at the moment.

"Hey! Happy New Year! Where's Liam? Did you guys share a New Year's kiss?" Lindsey teases, raising her eyebrows with a smirk.

"No. He left," I say, grabbing her champagne glass and downing it in one gulp.

"He... *left*? Why? What happened?" she asks, her voice full of surprise.

"Well," I say, taking Bailey's glass next and draining that too, "when I asked him why he'd been avoiding me all week after I kissed him at his family's Winter Solstice party, he told me the last girl he was in love with *died* and that it was somehow his fault. Oh! and that he might be in love with me. Still trying to decipher that last part."

They both stare at me, stunned. They exchange a look before leading me into the bedroom, quietly closing the door behind us.

I sit on the edge of the bed, my head spinning from all the champagne—and probably from everything with Liam as well.

"So… he told you?" Bailey asks cautiously.

"Yes. And my question is, why didn't any of you tell me from the start?" I ask, more hurt than angry. I don't like that I was left in the dark about this.

"Well… he asked us not to," Lindsey says gently, sitting beside me. Bailey leans against the dresser across the room.

"He did? When?" I ask, honestly surprised.

"The night you guys met, when we were all at O'Neill's," Bailey says.

"You two weren't exactly best friends back then," Lindsey adds. "We figured he wanted to tell you in his own time."

"But what about later? After we *did* become friends? We've gotten so close these past few months. Why wouldn't he tell me that his girlfriend died?" I ask, still trying to make sense of it all.

"Actually…" Bailey starts, hesitating. "She was his *wife.*"

I whip my head around to look at him, my jaw dropping. Liam was *married*?

"I don't know why he didn't tell you, Freya," Lindsey says softly. "And I wanted to. I really did. But it wasn't my story to tell."

I let out a heavy sigh. "I know. I'm not mad you didn't say anything. You were just being respectful. I just… I don't understand why he wouldn't want to tell me himself. *Especially* since he was married to her." I look down at my lap, the sadness starting to settle into something heavier.

"You need to talk to him," Lindsey says. "He has to be the one to tell you everything, especially now that things have gotten… complicated between you two." She pauses. "I can't believe you guys kissed. Why didn't you tell me?"

"I don't know. It was all so weird. He ended it so abruptly and asked me to leave without really giving me a reason. Although… I guess I know the reason now." I press my palms into my forehead. "I mean, of *course* he didn't want to make out with me when he's clearly still grieving his dead wife."

I groan, the guilt crashing in. "When did it happen? How did it happen?"

"It was a year and a half ago. Last June, she—" Bailey begins, but Lindsey cuts him off.

"You should really talk to Liam, Freya. *He* needs to be the one to tell you the story," she says pointedly, shooting Bailey a warning look. He shrugs, conceding.

"Yeah… no, you're right. I'm sorry for asking. I *will* talk to him. He just left so fast, I didn't even get the chance." I shake my head. "But that's probably for the best. He was really upset. God, I feel awful for pushing him like that. He's going to hate me now."

"No, he won't," Lindsey says firmly. "You had a right to know, and he knows that."

She pauses, then adds, "Look… all I can say is what I've been saying this whole time. You two *have* something between you. And whatever it is, I think it's worth exploring. Don't let either of your pasts get in the way of something that could be really amazing."

She gives me a small, knowing smile. "What he went through was really fucking awful. But I see the way he looks at you. I think you're helping him get back to the old Liam. And he's helped *you* get back to your old self, too."

I nod slowly and let out a long, shaky breath.

This time, I'm not too proud to admit it. Lindsey's right.

I have to talk to Liam.

***

It takes me a few minutes to muster up all my courage before I ring the doorbell. When I finally press the button, a fresh wave of anxiety washes through my whole body. I really hope I'm making the right decision by coming here.

A few seconds pass before the door swings open, and I'm face-to-face with Paula.

"Oh. Freya. It's nice to see you again," she says with a small but genuine smile. She doesn't seem surprised that I'm here.

"Hi, Paula. You too. How was the rest of your holiday?" I ask, awkwardly making small talk because I have no idea what else to say.

"It was nice, thank you. Come inside. Quickly, before you freeze out there." She waves me in. I'm grateful for the invitation; honestly, I wasn't sure I would get one.

"I know why you're here. But I'm not sure if he wants to talk right now. He's been holed up in his old bedroom upstairs since yesterday," Paula says as she takes my coat.

I tried countless times to get in touch with Liam on New Year's Day. I even went by his apartment when he wouldn't return my calls, but he wasn't there. That's how I figured out he must be at his parents' house. I know I might be overstepping by coming here, but I don't care anymore. I want to be there for him, no matter how he feels about me. And I need to know what happened to his wife.

"I don't mean to intrude. And if you want me to leave, I will. But... I would really like to talk to him," I say, giving her a pleading look.

"I know you do. And honestly, I think you might be the only one who *can* talk to him right now," Paula says earnestly. She pulls me into a hug, and I close my eyes, soaking in her tenderness. Her hugs really do feel like magic.

"Up the stairs, turn to your right. Last door on your left," she says simply as she loosens her embrace and leaves me to go see her son. As she starts down the hallway toward the kitchen, I whisper a soft thank you. She turns slightly to give me a little nod and a wave as if to say *you're welcome, now go on.* It's all the encouragement I need.

I look at the staircase and start to make my way up slowly.

When I reach the top, I follow Paula's directions and turn down the hall to my right. The last door on the left grows closer and closer with every step, until I'm finally standing in front of it. I lift my fist and gently knock three times on the wood. I wait.

After a few seconds, the door swings open, and a tired, tousled-looking Liam stands before me. He's wearing a blue *Salem State* sweatshirt with gray joggers. His hair doesn't look like it's been brushed today, and there are noticeable bags under his eyes, which tells me he hasn't gotten much sleep. He looks exactly like he did the morning after Lindsey's birthday dinner, when he showed up on my doorstep. But now it's me showing up at his door.

"Hi," I say softly. "May I come in?"

He looks at me silently for a moment before stepping to the side and opening the door a little wider so I can enter.

The bedroom is exactly what you'd expect from a grown-up child's room, preserved in its original state at their parents' house. Band posters hang on the walls, and high school memorabilia is displayed on every surface. One photo on his dresser—of him and Bailey in their freshman-year dorm—catches my eye as I walk past it. They both look so young.

Liam walks to the window, looking out at the front yard as I sit down on the edge of his bed and glance up at him. When he turns around and sees I've taken a seat, he slowly comes to sit beside me.

"Tell me what happened," I say quietly after a few moments, watching him.

He continues staring out the window. A heavy silence settles over the room. After what feels like an eternity, he sighs and begins his story.

"Her name was Suzana. And she was everything to me when I first fell in love with her. I met her in Manhattan, actually. I was finishing my graduate degree at a school in upstate New York at the time, and we met at a bar in the city. Almost exactly five years ago now, which seems crazy." He pauses as if it hurts to say the words.

"It all happened so fast. Too fast, now that I look back. After I graduated with my master's, I asked her to marry me. We had only been together for about five months. It was hasty, I know that now. But at the time, it just felt...

right. I really loved her. And I think she loved me, even though we didn't really know each other at all." Again, the words seem hard for him to get out.

"We eloped. My mom was furious, especially since she hadn't met her yet, and I was only twenty-five. She wanted me to experience life before I tied myself down. I probably should have listened.

"I wanted to come back to Massachusetts. I missed my family and friends, and I had a job lined up with the tour company. She agreed to move, since she didn't have anything keeping her in New York. Most of her family was dead, and she didn't have a strong connection to the city, anyway. So I brought her to Salem. I really thought it would work. At first, it did. She settled in, got a job, and met my friends and family. I was happy. Or maybe I kept trying to trick myself into thinking I was."

He pauses, and I wait with bated breath.

"Suzana didn't believe in any of the stuff my family does. She wasn't religious or spiritual, but it was more than just not believing. She sort of stuck her nose up at it, thought she was too good for it. I tried so many times to explain it to her, to get her to understand, but she never did. She thought Salem was crowded and corny. She thought my mom was crazy and my dad was annoying and loud." I close my eyes and sigh. Knowing how close Liam is to his family, I'm sure this must have hurt him.

He laughs softly. "For a while, I understood where she was coming from. It's hard to join a family like mine, especially when you don't come from a place that allows you to understand our beliefs. And I kind of dropped the ball explaining it when we first started dating."

This surprises me. Since the moment I met him, Liam has been nothing but proud of his religion and upbringing.

"You didn't tell her anything at all?" I ask.

He shakes his head. "I think I was terrified she'd judge me. That she'd leave me for it. So I never told her about Wicca or my ancestry or any of it. And then we got married, and by the time I brought her home, it was too late. I should've told her sooner. Maybe it would have made the transition easier. Because when I finally did explain, she reacted exactly how I feared."

A pang shoots through my heart.

"For three years, I pretended I didn't care when she made rude comments about family traditions. I ignored every eye roll when my father said a Pagan prayer at dinner. Every scoff when I brought home herbal tea my mother had given me. I didn't want to deal with it. I knew I'd made a mistake, and I didn't know how to get out of it."

He takes another long breath in.

"On the night she died, we were fighting, which honestly wasn't out of the ordinary for us at that point. We fought about everything. But this fight was different. It all started because she told me she didn't want us to see my family anymore. She didn't want to participate in their lives or holidays. She didn't want to live in Salem. And she certainly didn't want to raise children in our religion.

"I think out of everything, that was the biggest heartbreak of all for me. I can handle someone not liking me, I've got thick skin. But my family is the most important part of my life. So hearing that from someone I was supposed to spend the rest of my life with? Well, let's just say I didn't take it very well."

He stops for a long while, and it doesn't seem like he wants to continue. I take his hand in mine and give it a gentle squeeze. He looks down at our skin contact.

"What happened?" I ask softly. He swallows hard.

"We screamed at each other until our throats were raw. We both said things we could never take back, things I'll never repeat again. Eventually, she grabbed her keys and stormed out. I didn't stop her. I didn't want to. I was angry, but I still loved her. Or maybe... maybe I only loved the idea of her. The girl I fell for back in New York. She was the one I was holding onto. Like you said at the café a few months ago."

"You were still in love with the person you first fell for, not the person she became," I say. He nods.

"So when I got the call later that night that my wife had been hit by a semi-truck on Route 93... I went numb. And out of all the emotions I felt, guilt swallowed the rest. Guilt that it was my fault she left that night. Guilt that she probably crashed because she was so distracted after our fight.

"And guilt because, no matter how hard I tried, I couldn't shake the relief I felt when I hung up the phone. It's terrible, but it's the truth. At her funeral, I mourned a girl who didn't exist anymore, and a life with her that never would have been possible because she wouldn't have wanted to live it with me." He sniffles.

We sit in silence. I try to process everything, but before I can, he continues.

"When we first met, you reminded me of her. And I wanted to hate you for it. But I couldn't. There was this magnetic force pulling me toward you from the moment you bumped into me on that tour. I tried so hard to resist it. I ignored you. I said rude things. I was a complete jackass, just to keep you at arm's length. But the feeling never went away. And that scared the shit out of me. Because I couldn't risk being with someone like her again."

He takes a deep breath and looks at me for the first time since I sat down. There are crystals in his eyes.

"But you're not like her. Not one bit. Because you understand how special this town is to me. And you listen when I talk about Wicca. And you cried at The Witch Museum. And you celebrated the Winter Solstice. And you made the wreath with my mom and my aunt. And you danced with me. And you told me how much you loved celebrating with us.

"Every time you did one of those things, you gave me something she never could. You gave me hope. Hope that I could be accepted in a relationship. And wanted for who I am. And I really... *really* love you for that."

He keeps our eyes locked.

Once again, Liam has rendered me completely speechless. There are a million things I should say, and I will. But in that moment, I simply lean in and kiss him.

The kiss is tender and soft, nothing like the one we shared on the night of the Solstice. But honestly, I think I like this one better. We part for air after a moment, our foreheads resting together. His arms are wrapped loosely around my waist. My hands gently cup his cheeks. I wipe away the stray tear from his eyelashes.

"Thank you for telling me all of that. I appreciate it more than you know," I say sincerely, my own tears starting to form. He nods, gaze dipping slightly.

"I'm so sorry you went through all of this. I'm sorry your wife died. And I'm sorry she made you feel less than you are. You don't deserve that. Nobody deserves to feel alienated or inferior to their partner. Because that's not a partnership at all."

He sniffles again.

"Listen to me." I lift his chin, bringing his eyes to mine. "You're carrying so much guilt, and you don't need to. It's weighing on you, and you have to let it go. None of it was your fault, Liam. Not the fight. Not the crash. Not her inability to accept you or your family. *None* of it.

"It's okay to move on. And it's okay to cherish certain times with people you loved even if you end up falling out of love with them. Because at least you were able to have those good moments. Just because a relationship ends, it doesn't make that relationship a failure. It just means that you get to move on to the next one with new lessons learned." I say, realizing how much I should take my own advice.

Liam's eyes well with fresh tears.

"But if I let go of this guilt," he whispers, "then I'll feel like the worst person in the world. How can I move on so easily when my wife is dead? And I'm the one who's supposed to mourn her the most." He sounds so desperately hopeless.

"I don't think Suzana would want you to feel this way. It sounds like she had love for you, and you both knew the relationship wasn't working. You've been more than respectful. But honoring her shouldn't cost you your happiness. I think if she were still alive, she'd say the same."

I rub his back gently. He nods and looks down. I can tell from his breathing that he's struggling to keep it together.

"Thank you, Freya," he whispers after a minute. "For everything. You've helped me so much these past few months. Without even knowing it."

I nod, still rubbing his back. "I know I made you feel judged for your beliefs when we first met and I am so sorry for that. I hate that that's how I reacted, and I hope I didn't hurt you like Suzana did. I just didn't understand then. But I do now. Thanks to what you've taught me."

"I know. You didn't. I promise." Tears slip down his cheeks. His body shakes a little as he breathes in and I can tell he's still overthinking everything.

"I would never make you choose between me and your family." I say reassuringly. "Your family and your beliefs are part of what makes you, *you.* And I love you. Every piece. I would never take your pieces away."

When I finish, tears are streaming down my face. Liam looks at me like he's been waiting to hear those words his entire life. And finally, he lets go of his own tears completely. I pull him into a tight embrace. We couldn't get closer if we tried.

We hold each other for what feels like hours. His face is nuzzled into the space between my neck and shoulder. His body trembles with the occasional sob, and I just hold him and let him cry. I think it might be the first time he's ever let out this much emotion since Suzana's death. I want him to feel safe doing it.

At some point, we end up lying on his bed—me on my back, his head on my shoulder, one arm wrapped around my torso, half his body draped over mine. I keep my arms securely around him, reassuring him it'll all be okay.

Eventually, he cries himself to sleep. I gently move out from under him so he can get more comfortable. I pull the throw blanket over him, tiptoe quietly across the room, and close the door softly behind me as I leave.

Chapter 16

I reach the bottom of the stairs, and all I can think is that I need a strong cocktail. Or maybe I just need to sit for a moment and think. Rounding the left corner into the library, I expect to find the room empty, but instead, I see Paula sitting in one of the two armchairs that face the large bay window at the far end of the room. She's reading a book and sipping a cup of tea; the steaming pot rests on a tray on the small table to her right. When she hears me walk in, she turns and smiles.

"Sorry. I didn't mean to interrupt your reading," I say, turning to leave.

"No, no. It's okay, honey. Come and sit. I just brewed a fresh pot. Black tea for Saturday Magick," Paula says, placing her book down on her lap and turning to pour me some. I cautiously enter the room and take a seat in the chair opposite her. She hands me the small teacup, and I thank her. It's no whiskey, but I take a sip and decide that the tea will do. I should probably cut back on my drinking for the new year anyway.

"Where's Cadmun today?" I ask, not wanting to sit in silence for too long.

"He's helping Wells with a small construction project at my sister's house in Gloucester," Paula says, and I nod, taking another sip of tea. She doesn't speak again for another minute, but then finally breaks the silence.

"Are you okay?"

"I'm fine. It's Liam who I'm thinking about right now," I say with a shrug.

"But your feelings are equally as important. I assume he told you what happened." She says, and I nod again.

"I think I have a bit of emotional whiplash. I felt like I was getting so close to him these past few months. Like we were getting close to each other. And now… I feel like there are parts of him that I had no idea existed." I let my thoughts pour out of me. If I can't sit and think alone, then the next best option is to tell someone how I feel. And Paula is a great candidate for the job.

"That's what's great about a relationship. You continue to learn new things about the person every day. I'm still discovering things about Cadmun that I never knew before. It's what keeps everything fun after you've been together for so long," she says, giggling to herself a bit.

"But I just feel like our friendship has been built on a lie," I say truthfully.

"He should have told you. I know that. And he knows that, too. But he was scared. I don't think he's felt the way he feels about you for anyone else. Not even Suzana," she says, taking a sip of her tea.

"Well, I don't know about that—"

"It's true, Freya. I saw it at the Winter Solstice. I see it every time he mentions you in conversation. I think teaching you everything about Salem and his ancestry has been really cathartic for him. He's so passionate about how we raised him and our lineage, and he has always wanted to share that with someone he loves. I'm glad that he found you," she says, reaching over to squeeze my arm. I can't help but smile. Hearing all of that from Liam's mother puts everything into perspective.

"I am, too. I guess I'm just scared that I'm not the right person for him to move on with. That he should have fallen in love with someone else. I'm so bad at love and, honestly, I'm still healing from my own past. I don't want to put my baggage on top of his. It isn't fair to him."

Paula lets out a little laugh. "Oh, honey. You can't help who you fall in love with. It's all written in the stars. We just have to go along with what the universe has in store for us," she says, pouring herself a fresh cup of tea.

I laugh a little at her comment. "I wonder if my ex and I were written in the stars, too." It's meant to be a joke, but there's a layer of sincerity to my words.

"You might have been. And Liam and Suzana probably were as well. To teach you both the lessons you needed to continue on in your journey and find true love and happiness," she says simply. "Starting a relationship doesn't require both participants to be completely healed from their past traumas. The beauty of a relationship is that you can lean on each other and help each other heal and grow to become the people you're meant to be."

We sit in silence for another minute or two, and I can't help but admit to myself that she's right. I look over at her, and she looks over at me, and I give her a kind smile.

"Thank you, for everything. It's helpful to talk to you," I say genuinely.

"Of course, dear. It's what mothers are for," she says. I don't mention the fact that my mother and I have never had a conversation quite like this one. But I don't hold the same resentment I once would have about that. I know my mom gives me everything she is capable of giving. Instead, I just silently thank the universe that I found someone else to have these conversations with.

There's silence for a little while longer before Paula breaks it again.

"At the end of the day, you have to do what's right for you. But it would be a real shame if you didn't try something beautiful just because you're both afraid of demons in your pasts," she says, taking another sip of her tea. I realize that advice sounds familiar.

"Lindsey told me something very similar to that the other night," I say with a small smile.

"Smart girl," Paula says. I take a sip from my teacup and laugh to myself a little. Lindsey would be thrilled to hear a comment like that.

"Do you know where your name comes from?" Paula asks, seemingly out of the blue.

"No. I don't, actually." I'm immediately brought back to the day in the café when I told Liam about Jackson, and he asked me the same question. Somehow, I had completely forgotten about that conversation.

"Freya is the Norse goddess of love," she answers simply.

"Really?" I ask, slightly surprised.

"You see? How can you be bad at something that your own namesake ruled over? Now, you can call on her anytime you're having doubts or need a little help in the love department," Paula says with a small shrug and a smile.

I feel a chill snake down my body. How did I never know that was where my name came from? Suddenly, I feel this new vitality and warmth when I think about my name and its implications. I'm also starting to think Liam has known about this all along. Why wouldn't he have told me when he first asked?

"I think I will do that, actually. Thank you for telling me." I feel like I finally have my own tangible connection to the Pagan world.

"You're welcome," Paula says, starting to stand up from her seat. "Come with me, lovie. We're going to do a little Saturday ritual for protection for this coming week."

I stand up and follow her out of the room, a little intrigued by what she has planned.

***

"So, do I just…"

"Yep. Just light the candle and close your eyes," she says gingerly. "And then we'll meditate for spiritual protection and protection for the household."

"Okay," I say with a small smile. I strike the match and light the tall black candle sitting in a little bowl of salt. According to Paula, Saturdays are for blessings of protection against hostility and bad energy in both your home and your spirit. Honestly, I could use a little bit of that Magick, so I'm excited to do the ritual with her.

After I light the candle, we both close our eyes and sit for a few seconds in silence. Paula says that all I have to do to set the intention is picture bad energy leaving my space and good energy coming into it. So that's what I do.

I can see myself in my mind's eye, darkness fizzing away from me as light energy is absorbed into every inch of my body. A warmth washes over me as I picture this in my head. I'm still not sure I've got the whole Magick thing down yet. But at the very least, I can't deny I've noticed that even the smallest shift toward a positive mindset can make the hard days feel a little easier.

"All right, that should do it!" Paula says after about a minute. I open my eyes and smile at her across the table.

"Thank you for including me in this, Paula. The more I learn about Wicca, the more I really enjoy the practice," I say earnestly.

"You are more than welcome to join us anytime," she says with a smile. And I think I will take her up on the offer. She's very accepting of people who aren't like her, and I really appreciate that. I could learn a lot from her, honestly.

As Paula stands up from her chair and blows out the candle, I feel a presence appear at the doorway of the kitchen to my right. I turn my head to see Liam crossing the threshold with a worried look on his face. When he locks his eyes onto mine, his shoulders visibly sag and his face relaxes instantly.

"I thought you left," he says, sounding a little dejected.

"Oh. No, I'm still here. I've just been hanging out with your mom," I say with a chuckle, gesturing to Paula.

"I'll leave you kids to talk," she says, passing by Liam and giving his shoulder a little pat as she leaves the room. Liam gives her a small smile as she passes, then looks back over at me.

"Wanna go on a walk?" he asks.

I smile and nod. "Okay."

*****

The full moon is out tonight, its silver light paving the way beneath our feet. We head toward the water, down the dead-end road that his parents' house sits atop. So far, neither of us has said a word. But that's okay. It's just pleasant to be in each other's company. There's no tension in the air. No emotions left unsaid. We both know how the other feels, and there's a certain level of security in that knowledge.

"I'm sorry I broke down like that. I'm not usually that emotional," Liam says with a hint of humor. I smile at that, because I know he must be feeling a bit better.

"You don't have to apologize. You've let me cry out all my emotions so many times, it's only fair I return the favor," I joke, though I honestly would never turn down an opportunity to comfort him. He throws me a small smile, and we walk in silence for a few more minutes until Liam speaks again.

"You did the Saturday blessing with my mom." It's more of a statement than a question.

"Mm-hmm. I really enjoyed it," I say, thinking for another moment. "Did you know my name comes from the Norse goddess of love?" I ask, though I'm pretty sure I know the answer.

He laughs. "Yes. I did."

"Why did you pretend like you didn't?" I ask.

"I was waiting for you to discover it on your own. I didn't want to tell you because I wanted you to find your own path to Paganism. I knew you would, when the timing was right," he says simply. And I understand.

We reach the end of the street, and there's nowhere else to go except to turn around and walk back. But we don't do that. Instead, we stand silently, looking out across the vast ocean before us and the sky's horizon beyond it. There's still one question weighing on my mind, and I have to ask it before we talk about anything else.

"Why didn't you tell me before?" I know he'll understand what I mean.

He sighs. "I meant to. I'm sorry I let so much time pass before talking about it. But I just—I liked that you didn't see me as the broken guy with the mean, dead wife. You saw me as just some regular person who may be a little rough around the edges and a bit too stubborn for his own good sometimes." He lets out a small chuckle before continuing. "Eventually, it got to the point where I felt like it was too late to say anything. I didn't want you to feel how you're probably feeling right now—betrayed and lied to. I never want you to feel like that, and I swear I'll never keep anything from you again. I'm just not always the best at telling people how I'm feeling the moment that I feel it."

I look out to the water and mull over his response for a while. And I get it. Honestly, I'm not even mad at him. Unfortunately, I think I might love him too much to stay mad at him about anything for too long.

"I'm sorry I didn't turn out the way you thought I would," he says after a second, kicking a rock with his foot.

I sigh, still gazing out at the horizon. "None of us do in the end, really. Just as long as you continue to show me the inner parts of you as they grow and change… I'll be happy." There's another long pause, and I let out a little chuckle when a thought crosses my mind.

"What?" Liam asks.

"Nothing. I just think it's funny we were both in Manhattan at the same time. You never mentioned you went to school in the area."

"I was mostly upstate. I only ever went into the city to see Suzana, and she came up to where I was more often. She was a bartender in the Village, so she had a pretty flexible schedule."

"Was that the bar you met her at?" I ask curiously.

"Yep. Actually, the night we met, I was supposed to be meeting a blind date, but the girl never showed up. I found out later I was given the wrong meeting time, but it didn't matter, I guess, because I ended up talking to Suzana all night. Sometimes I wonder what would've happened if I'd actually gone on that blind date, though. How things might have been different."

My eyebrows scrunch a bit as I process his words. My brain reels for a moment as I flash back to five years ago and realize something.

"Wait. Was the bar White Oak Tavern?"

A look of surprise shows on Liam's face. "Yeah, how did you know that?"

"Were you set up on the date by your friend Tom from grad school?" The words rush out of my mouth as two and two connect in my head.

Liam's eyes widen. "Yes. How could you possibly—"

"It was me," I say, half to Liam and half to myself, looking out at the horizon as the realization flows over me. "It was me. I was the one you were supposed to meet at the bar. I was the one you were being set up with." I turn to look at him again. Our eyes meet, and both our expressions are ones of pure shock. "It was me."

I feel an electrifying tingle pass through my entire body.

"But… but how did—I…" Liam stammers, trying to form his thoughts into words. "You were *Stacy's* friend?" he finally asks, incredulously.

"Yes! And I waited for you to show up, and you never did. And that was the night that Jackson and I first got together," I blurt out, as if I've just found the answer to a deep secret I've been searching for my whole existence.

The last five years of my life whirl around me, like a movie montage, flashing scene after scene. Memories resurrect in my head of me and Jackson together—memories that may never have happened if I had met Liam that night.

I'm absolutely stunned. How could it have been me?

Suddenly, Liam starts to laugh. I look over at him, and a huge smile slowly spreads across my face. I start giggling along with him. Soon we're both reduced to cackles, gasping for air, tears streaming down my cheeks. This time, though, they're happy tears. Ecstatic ones.

"Well, I was not expecting that," he says after a couple of minutes, as we both calm down and find our normal breaths again.

"Me either," I say with a smile, shaking my head in disbelief as I look up at the moon.

Everything feels so serendipitous. Like my whole life has led up to this day. Discovering the meaning of my name and then discovering the truth about my lost blind date five years ago. It all feels like it's been made up for a play or a movie. But it wasn't. It's real.

Were we destined to find each other? Were we brought together by the positive intentions I set on Halloween or the Winter Solstice? Or are we just two fools who happened to fall in love? Maybe it's a combination of all three. I don't know.

But I don't think it was a coincidence that we were meant to meet all those years ago. Maybe the universe knew we needed to each learn our own lessons before we could come together fully. At that thought, Paula's words ring through my head. *It's all written in the stars.*

"Freya," Liam says. I look back over at him. His green eyes pierce mine, and I feel that electricity that seems to be our constant companion now. "I want to make this work. I want to be with you. And if you'll take me for the stubborn, avoidant asshole that I am… then I promise I will love you for the rest of my life. And for all the lives that I live after it."

I stare at him for a moment. Once again, he's telling me something with his eyes. And I know the message behind them now. *It's love.* The message was always love. He's been trying to tell me all along. I smile at that thought.

"You have a beautiful smile. Have I ever told you that?" he adds absentmindedly, before I can say anything.

"Really? Some guy once told me the gap in my teeth makes me spit when I talk," I respond with a smirk.

"Well, that guy probably had a pretty big stick up his ass, so I wouldn't worry about him." I chuckle, and he pauses for a moment, his eyes flicking down to my chest, where the rose quartz necklace he gave me peeks out beneath my coat.

"…So you accept?"

I sigh and purse my lips, feigning as though I'm contemplating my decision, but I know he can see right through me. "I guess I do," I say.

"You guess, huh? Y'know, Blondie, you may be just as stubborn as I am."

I smirk. "Oh boy. Then this is gonna be fun." At that, I jump into his arms and wrap mine around his neck, kissing him for the second time today. He pulls me tightly into him, holding me close, as if he'll never let me go. Not that I'd ever want him to. Not now. Not ever.

Epilogue

Two years later

"Can I take these treats out to everyone?" I ask Paula as she begins to make yet another batch of Wassail for the evening.

"Oh, yes, lovie! That would be great. Thank you!" she says, giving my shoulder a squeeze.

I pick up the tray and push the back kitchen door open, heading out to the yard. The Yule log is already blazing strong, courtesy of the Doyle boys and the helping hands they had from Bailey and Damon.

"Who wants sweets?" I shout to everyone sitting around the fire pit. They all turn at the sound of my voice, but of course, Damon is the first to reach me.

"I can take this off your hands, Freya dear," he says in a mockingly sweet tone, taking the tray from me.

"All right, fine. But you have to share, Damon!" I yell after him as he carries the entire tray back to his bench, already snacking on one of the desserts. I laugh as I watch the girls descend on him like a pack of lionesses who've just scoped out their next prey.

Liam and Bailey are sitting on the other side of the fire pit, chatting with Cadmun and Uncle Wells. I smile happily, watching everyone gathered together, joyfully celebrating the holiday.

It's been two years. Two years since the first time I celebrated the Winter Solstice with Liam's family. Two years since we discovered how truly intertwined our lives were. And two years since I fell in love with the best man I have ever known. My love for him hasn't dwindled one bit. In fact, it's grown an infinite amount—if that's even possible.

I'm pulled from my thoughts when Paula and Aunt Maureen come barreling through the back door with more trays of desserts and another pot of Wassail.

"Everyone! More goodies!" Maureen shouts, and I follow in their path toward the food table we set up to the right of the fire pit.

As I start to pour myself another mugful of the delicious beverage, Liam sneaks up behind me and wraps his arms around my waist.

"Everything okay?" I ask, looking over my shoulder with a smile.

"Mm-hmm. Just needed to get a little warm," he hums sweetly. I giggle, squeezing his arms that remain around me, and take a sip from my cup.

"You two are just adorable," Charlene says as she comes up beside us to grab more Wassail for herself and Jenna. "I guess it's a good thing neither of you ever considered going out with any of the people I tried to set you up with. Even though they were all excellent matches, not that you would know," she teases, and we both laugh.

"Well, Damon's still single. So you can put your incredible matchmaking skills to good use on him," I say, gesturing to Damon, who is somehow coming over for more desserts.

"That's true. I do have a few people that could work for you, actually," Charlene contemplates with a little grin.

"Oh, no need. I'm seeing someone new. Her name's Elle and she's a yoga instructor. I swear, I'm gonna marry this one," Damon says proudly.

Liam snorts. "You said the same thing about Amy two years ago."

"…Who's Amy?" Damon asks, a confused look on his face.

"Never mind," Liam says, shaking his head as he finally lets me go so he can refill his own mug.

Celebrating the Pagan holidays with Liam's family has become the norm for me over the past couple of years. We dance around the Maypole for Beltane in the spring. For Samhain in the fall, we build an altar for loved ones who have passed. And we gather for all the other holidays in between, giving thanks to life and praying for luck and prosperity as the seasons change.

But my favorite celebration is still the one we have for the Winter Solstice on December 21st.

Tomorrow, Liam and I are flying to New York for Christmas with my parents. I've grown closer to them over the past couple of years, even with the distance between us. And with Liam by my side, visits home have become a lot easier, especially since my family has embraced him so wholeheartedly. There was definitely a learning curve when they found out he was Wiccan—they are *my* family, after all—but I was able to help guide them through it, drawing on my own personal experiences. They've even visited Salem a few times now.

"Liam! Now, look at this. You see, this is a nice mustache," Bailey says, batting Liam's shoulder and gesturing to Wells' face, where he has allowed his facial hair to grow out. "Don't you think I'd look good with one of those?"

"Yeah, sure. Why don't you grow one?" Liam asks, draping his arm around my shoulders.

"Lindsey won't let me before the wedding," Bailey pouts.

"Oh God, who's gotten him started on the mustache again?" Lindsey shouts from the other side of the fire pit, where she sits with Charlene and Jenna.

Liam puts his hands up defensively. "Wasn't me, I swear." He still receives a glare from her, though.

I laugh and squeeze Liam's arm, then leave his warm embrace and round the fire to the other side. I take a seat on the bench next to Lindsey and the girls.

"Okay, let me just see the ring one more time," I say excitedly. She laughs and removes her glove before extending her left hand so all four of us can gaze upon the beautiful rock. The very large, beautiful rock. Bailey has good taste, I must say.

"I'd lie and tell you that I'm tired of showing it off to people. But I'm not," Lindsey says with a shrug and a smirk, still admiring her hand.

I sit and chat with the girls as we all drink from our warm mugs. A few minutes later, Cadmun and Uncle Wells grab their instruments and begin to play some Celtic music, as they have for the past two years on this day. Bailey and Lindsey are the first to start dancing. Then Charlene and Jenna follow, and Damon offers his partnering services to Paula and Maureen.

Eventually, I feel a tap on my shoulder and swing around to be met with my ever-reliable dancing partner.

"May I have this dance?" Liam asks, his hand extended for me to take.

"You may," I say with a smile.

He leads me to the open space next to the fire pit and pulls me into an embrace that we've become so familiar with now. Over the past two years, there have been so many other dances, I wouldn't even be able to count them all. But my favorites still remain the ones we share on the Solstice.

We stare into each other's eyes as we sway to the music, passing messages of love back and forth through our gaze.

"I'll never get tired of dancing with you," I say after a few minutes.

"Well, give it a few decades. That may change," Liam quips with a chuckle.

I shake my head. "No, it never will. I fell in love with you during our first dance. And I fall more and more in love with you with every dance after it," I conclude with a smile.

Liam leans down and connects our lips in a kiss. We continue to sway to the melody as we kiss, slowly and tenderly. When we pull away, his eyes drift down to my chest, where the rose quartz necklace he gave me two years ago still rests. He reaches up and gently takes the stone into his grasp, rolling it between his fingers.

"You said it would help me find love and happiness," I say, looking down at the crystal.

"I did," he says, placing the necklace back against my chest and letting our eyes meet again. "I'm glad it led you to me."

If there are two things I've learned living in Salem, Massachusetts, for the past two and a half years, it's that true magic can be found anywhere, if you give it a chance.

And I am still, and forever will be, head over heels for Liam Cadmun Fucking Doyle.

The End.

Dear Reader,

If you're seeing this message, then I owe you a massive THANK YOU! Because it probably means you just read my debut novel. Or, it means you skipped to the very back of the book… and if that's the case, I urge you to flip to the front and start reading!

It has been almost two years since I first sat down and decided to write Witch City: Salem in Love, and I'm absolutely over the moon that it's finally in readers' hands. I never thought I'd be capable of writing an entire book… but here we are, and I'm still in awe.

Salem has always been a special place to me, and I think it's often misunderstood. I wrote this story because I believe its history deserves to be shared and its people celebrated. And what better way to do that than by making a judgy New Yorker fall in love with a practicing Salem Wiccan, right in the heart of the Witch City itself?

Of course, I could never have done this alone. Thank you to everyone who supported me throughout this journey and helped me get this book to where it is today, but especially...

Emma and **Connie**—you were the first two people to read the earliest draft of this book, and your encouragement gave me the push to keep going. I truly can't thank you enough.

Victoria—you helped me shape Freya into who she is. Without your editorial insight and guidance, I would have been completely lost.

And finally, **you**—thank you for taking a chance on this book and on me. I'm so lucky to count you as a reader, and I hope you'll stick around for future projects.

If you enjoyed Witch City: Salem in Love, please consider leaving a review. They help indie authors more than you know, and I'd appreciate it forever!

And of course, be sure to subscribe to my email newsletter to stay up to date on new releases and news. You can sign up here at juliac123.substack.com.

Thank you again, and happy reading!

With gratitude,

Julia

Selected Sources & Further Reading

"The Journey from 1692 to Salem's Modern Witch Community." Destination Salem.
https://www.salem.org/which-witch/the-journey-from-1692-to-salems-modern-witch-community/

"Paganism." Encyclopaedia Britannica.
https://www.britannica.com/topic/paganism

"The Salem Witch Trials of 1692." Peabody Essex Museum.
https://www.pem.org/the-salem-witch-trials-of-1692

"How Did the Salem Witch Trials End?" Encyclopaedia Britannica.
https://www.britannica.com/question/How-did-the-Salem-witch-trials-end

History.com Editors. "Salem Witch Trials: Justice and Legal Legacy." HISTORY.
https://www.history.com/news/salem-witch-trials-justice-legal-legacy

Rothschild, Amanda. "It Took 300 Years, But Salem Finally Cleared the Last Witch's Name." NBC News, 2022. https://www.nbcnews.com/think/amp/rcna54444

"8 Ways to Celebrate Yule." Cosmic Drifters. https://cosmicdrifters.com/8-ways-to-celebrate-yule-happy-winter-solstice/

Rowbotham, Jill. "The History of the Christmas Tree." ABC News Australia, 2016. https://www.abc.net.au/news/2016-12-19/the-history-of-the-christmas-tree/8106078

Thomas, Roya Backlund. "Winter Solstice Rituals to Try This Year." StyleCaster. https://stylecaster.com/lifestyle/zodiac/1241990/winter-solstice-rituals/

Berger, Helen. "Understanding Wicca in the Modern World." Brandeis University. https://www.brandeis.edu/now/2021/september/wicca-berger-conversation.html

Wicca Handbook. Federal Bureau of Prisons. https://www.bop.gov/foia/docs/wiccamanual.pdf

"Wicca Religious Accommodations." Washington State Department of Corrections. https://www.doc.wa.gov/docs/publications/infographics/100-PO047.htm

"The Origins and Practices of Samhain, Día de los Muertos, and All Saints' Day." Boston Public Library. https://www.bpl.org/blogs/post/the-origins-and-practices-of-holidays-samhain-dia-de-los-muertos-and-all-saints-day/

"Bridget Bishop Home and Orchards." Salem Witch Museum. https://salemwitchmuseum.com/locations/bridget-bishop-home-and-orchards-site-of/

"Saturday Magic: Rituals & Spells." Spells8. https://spells8.com/saturday-magic-spells/

"Freyja." Encyclopaedia Britannica. https://www.britannica.com/topic/Freyja

"Who Is Freya?" NorthernPaganism.org. https://www.northernpaganism.org/shrines/freya/who-is-freya.html

"10 Crystals for Happiness." Conscious Items. https://consciousitems.com/blogs/practice/crystals-for-happiness

"Magick." Pluralism Project, Harvard University. https://pluralism.org/magick

"The Salem Lyceum." Ghost City Tours.
https://ghostcitytours.com/salem/haunted-places/lyceum-salem/

"Salem Lyceum Hall History." Salem Ghosts.
https://salemghosts.com/salem-lyceum-hall/

"Quantum Physics and Spirituality." Mind That Ego.
https://www.mindthatego.com/quantum-physics-and-spirituality/

Sinha, Pritam Kumar. "Quantum Mechanics and Spiritual Consciousness." Medium.
https://medium.com/@pritamkumarsinha/quantum-mechanics-and-spiritual-consciousness-navigating-the-confluence-of-science-and-mysticism-b693244541cf